“Would you brothers think in me?”

Lilah’s breath came out in a whisper as a pounding sounded at the door. “I’ve had it with their tireless campaign to marry me off.”

Tyler nodded understanding, and with one swift move he unfastened the top two buttons of her modest blouse, exposing a good two inches of skin. He reached up and loosened his tie and yanked open the top button of his own shirt.

“Tyler?” Her voice quivered.

“Shh, angel,” he said, then lowered his lips to hers. Lilah’s breath froze in her throat as the sensation of being expertly kissed by Tyler Westlake hit her.

When he released Lilah, her lips felt as if they belonged to another woman; her lipstick was no doubt smudged, her hair no longer neatly combed.

“Go let your brother in, angel.” he finally said in a low, raspy voice, “and tell him that if he has any men to send round this evening, he’s wasting his time. You’re already taken tonight.”

Myrna Mackenzie, winner of the Holt Medallion honouring outstanding literary talent, has always been fascinated by the belief that within every man is a hero, and inside every woman lives a heroine. She loves to write about ordinary people making extraordinary dreams come true. A former teacher, Myrna lives in the suburbs of Chicago with her husband—who was her high school sweetheart—and her two sons. She believes in love, laughter, music, vacations to the mountains, watching the stars, anything unattached to the words *physical fitness*, and letting dustballs gather where they may. Readers can write to Myrna at PO Box 225, LaGrange, IL, 60525-0225, USA.

Recent titles by the same author:

AT THE BILLIONAIRE'S BIDDING
THE BILLIONAIRE IS BACK

BLIND-DATE BRIDE

BY

MYRNA MACKENZIE

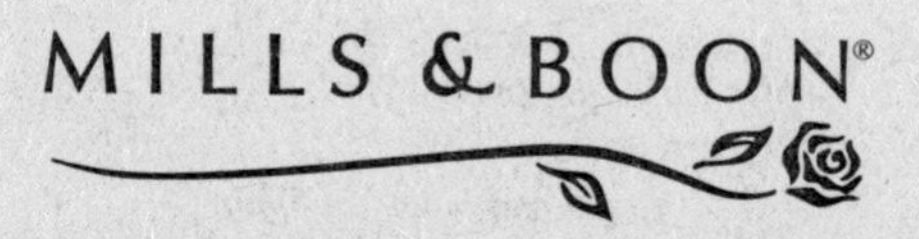

First published in Great Britain 2002
Harlequin Mills & Boon Limited,
Eton House, 18-24 Paradise Road, Richmond, Surrey TW9 1SR

ISBN 0 263 82967 7

Set in Times Roman 10½ on 12 pt.
01-0902-46464

Printed and bound in Spain
by Litografia Rosés, S.A., Barcelona

Chapter One

The sound of frantic lover-like whispering caught Tyler Westlake's attention, and he shifted his stance and shrugged. It wasn't every day that a man was treated to lovers' trysts in a bookshop in broad daylight, but then, this was a tourist town. Lots of people were here simply to play, and anyway, he'd taken women into his arms in even less circumspect places.

Tyler smiled at the admission. It wasn't his business to judge or even to notice. Besides which, he had other things on his mind right now, information to locate, lots of work to accomplish and not much time to do it in. He spared a glance at his Rolex. Getting sidetracked by thoughts of passion and a woman's soft body wasn't on the schedule. At least not this morning.

Tyler went back to perusing the research book he'd been thinking might be useful, determined not to heed the couple in the next aisle.

''Lilah, come on,'' a man's voice cajoled. The bookcase shook. A woman squeaked.

''John, listen to me. Don't do this, please. I like you, and you're a good man, but—'' The woman's voice was low and honeyed and slightly distressed. The pitch of her whispering rose at the end, becoming a tiny bit more forceful. A thud sounded as a book fell off the shelf.

Tyler shifted his own book in his hands. He raised one brow.

''Oh, I know you like me, Lilah,'' a man's voice said, his tone overly slick and confident. ''Everyone likes me. I'm one of the good guys. That's why your brother knew we'd be a good match, you and I. There are plenty of women who want me. You could, in fact, do a heck of a lot worse than to marry me. Everybody thinks so.''

The words drifted over and Tyler couldn't help wondering just who ''everybody'' was, because this guy had the kind of I'm-always-right voice that made a man want to plant a fist dead in the center of his face. Still, Tyler concentrated on keeping his hands right on the book where they belonged. He didn't even know these people, so while he might think any woman would have to be a fool to give in to a man with an attitude like that, it wasn't really any of his affair. Even if the woman had a raw-silk voice that made him itch to step around the corner and see if she had a face to match that sultry angel's whisper.

''I'm sorry if you were misled somehow,'' she said. ''I don't know what my brother Hank told you, but I'm just not—I'm not actively looking for a husband right now. I'm flattered that you should ask, but I really can't accept your offer. Oh no, don't do that. Really, think about what you're doing, and please…don't. No,'' the woman said, and Tyler's good intentions went sailing down the street. He tossed his book down. He swung around the corner, his long legs carrying him to the next aisle in several quick strides.

The scene that greeted him brought him to a halt.

A pretty, tawny-haired woman was backed up against a bookshelf, a heavy tome in hand as if she meant to hit the man kneeling before her if he came any closer. The man was holding a bunch of weedy flowers in one hand. The hem of the lady's pale pink skirt was crunched into his other palm, tethering her to him. He turned at that moment, a cockeyed grin on his face.

"Don't mind us," he said. "I'm proposing to the lady here. We were just getting to know each other better."

The woman's midnight-blue eyes flashed silver sparks. Her long, golden-brown hair swung out gently as she shook her head. "John, I've *known* you most of my life, and we've always been friends, but I absolutely don't understand what's gotten into you. Really. You're just going to have to leave my store now. What will my customers think? Please get up and—and give me my skirt back." She glanced up into Tyler's eyes, and he felt a vague sense of déjà vu. He'd seen this woman before, in the days when he used to visit Sloane's Cove, Maine, as a boy. He was sure of it. There was just something about her....

Whatever it was, she had turned her attention to him at that moment. Those great blue eyes were studying him imploringly, her cheeks had turned a most luscious shade of rose, and she was clutching the book even harder than before. Tyler had the distinct impression that she was wishing that one of them, either she or he, would disappear at that moment. He was sorry to have to tell her that it wasn't going to be him. Especially since she appeared to be in a no-win situation, and also since he had no sense that she might have any truly deep feelings for the grinning, muscled, overconfident idiot in front of her. Like it or not, busy or not, Tyler just couldn't walk away from a woman being backed into a corner by someone twice her size.

As Tyler stared at her, her blush deepened slightly. She looked down, long lashes hiding those spectacular eyes from him.

"We're done here. Please let me out now, John," she said again in a gentle but commanding voice.

"Lilah, you're already past the age when most women around here have had their first babies. I have two kids, ready made, and I need someone to help me manage them. You'd be good for them." He tugged on her hem a bit more, and the fabric slipped a fraction.

Tyler tried not to notice what nicely curved legs the lady had, but then hell, he'd never been anything near a saint, and they really were incredible legs. Long, pale, bare. The kind of legs that made a man want to slip off those wisps of high-heeled sandals she was wearing and stroke his hands over her skin. Very, very slowly. For a second he could almost manage to feel sorry for the arrogant fool the lady was doing her best to let down easy. Almost, but not quite. The man was, after all, trying to force himself on her when she'd already said no, and that kind of thing had never played well with Tyler.

He took a step forward. His movement registered with the persistent suitor, who turned and frowned at him. "You still here? Hit the road, buddy. You're not wanted."

Tyler wondered for a second if the man was right.

He probably *wasn't* wanted, and interfering in other people's lives had never been his way. He was very much a "live and let live" kind of man, a good thing when his own relationships were by choice, short, purely physical, and not bound by society's more-conventional rules. His own life couldn't stand much scrutiny in certain areas, and no doubt about it, he should absolutely bow out and mind his own business; but then, the little beauty was showing clear signs of agitation in her lovely blue eyes. People were starting to gather, and she gave a slight tug on her skirt.

"Sorry, but I'm not going anywhere just yet," Tyler said carefully, casually propping himself against a nearby bookcase. "There's a book on the shelf behind you that I happen to need."

The man on the ground simply growled and turned his attention back to the woman. The lady, however, actually raised one brow as she glanced at the shelf Tyler had indicated. Books on crocheting lace doilies were prominently displayed.

Tyler coughed and grinned slightly. He didn't bother moving.

The errant suitor edged nearer the woman.

She pressed herself closer against the bookshelf behind her. She looked down at the man, sadness and determination coloring her expression.

"I'm genuinely sorry, John, if Hank led you to believe that I was looking. I'm sure you're anxious for your children, but you...I, it's just not a solution. For either of us." The woman reached for his hand to pull his fingers away. When she did, the man let go of her skirt and grabbed her hand, pulling her toward him a bit, persistently tugging.

"I could change your mind, Lilah. I've changed

women's minds before. I could convince you to like me more than you do. You turn me down now, I can't guarantee I'm going to ask again. You keep this up for too many more years, no man will even be asking anymore.''

He tugged harder, and she nearly lost her balance.

Embarrassed distress registered in the lady's eyes.

Tyler cleared his voice. ''Darn, I hate to interrupt you again just when you were really turning on the charm full force,'' he told the man who was now scowling at the woman, ''but I could definitely use some help finding the right book, and I'm hoping that this lady can help me. Perhaps you might consider doing your wooing in a more private place next time,'' he told the man. ''Could be something to think about.''

''This is Lilah's store,'' the man said with a disgruntled frown, as if Tyler hadn't been there to hear her mention that very fact just moments ago.

''That's good news, then. I've come to the right place, but it *does* appear that the lady would like her hand back,'' Tyler noted. ''It's not exactly fair to use force against someone so much tinier than you, now, is it, my friend?'' He eased away from the shelf and slowly moved toward the man, glad that nature had granted him the gift of height and shoulders and a pair of glittering green eyes that made him look kin to the devil. ''It might be a good idea to let her go right about now. I'm sure you can find a more suitable place to ask a woman to marry you. It may have escaped your attention, but you seem to have attracted an audience,'' Tyler said, nodding toward a few people peeking around the bookshelves and those whose noses were pressed to the window looking in. The bell on the door rang softly and several more people piled inside.

As if he'd finally realized that he was getting nowhere, the man swore and let go of the woman's hand. He began to rise to his feet.

"Lilah's good at playing cat and mouse," he complained.

"Then I guess you should look for another mouse," Tyler conceded. "Preferably a willing one."

As the man stomped away and out of the store, Tyler raised one lazy, knowing brow, assessing the people peeking around the corner and through the window, and they shuffled away. He turned back then, his eyes meeting those of the woman he'd tried to protect, and he smiled slightly. "Are you all right?"

She nodded, and lifted one delicate shoulder, managing an apologetic smile. "John wouldn't really have hurt me. By tomorrow he'll probably feel guilty and come to apologize. He's just a bit intense and cranky these days since his wife divorced him. And my brothers—oh, well, it doesn't matter," she said with a slight shake of her head that sent her long hair brushing against the pale skin revealed by the V-neck of her white blouse. "I'm Lilah Austin, the owner of this shop," she said instead. "And you said you were looking for a book, Mr. Westlake. What kind?"

Tyler didn't bother asking how she knew who he was. His mother had lived here for many years before her death. He'd summered here himself many years ago, before he'd been sent away. The Westlake name was well known. It stood for money. It stood for notoriety, and her name, Lilah Austin, had finally registered. He remembered now. Lilah Austin, quiet, smart and about as painfully shy as a little girl could get. Her shyness had intrigued him, her pretty blushes when he said hello had entranced him. He remembered that she had a weakness for wildflowers and once he'd found her picking them at the edge of his mother's property. She'd looked so guilty and so lost and embarrassed, as if she wished she could replant the blossoms.

"It's all right," he'd told her, but she'd only blushed more, like some wild, lovely rose in human form.

Nowadays her voice was still low and quiet, though she wore an air of professional composure. Her slender hand was folded tightly against the belt at her waist, and he wondered how much of that composure was a mask, how hard she'd fought to overcome her basic shyness. He wondered if she still liked wildflowers. He also realized his silence and his scrutiny were making her nervous.

"Mr. Westlake? The book?" she repeated.

He shook his head, holding his hands out palm up. "I was just making conversation with the man," he admitted. "It seemed the thing to do at the time."

"I—yes, I guess it was the thing to do," she said. "Thank you, Mr. Westlake. If you're sure that you don't need anything from me—any help finding a book, I mean," she stammered, the sweet pink returning to her cheeks, "I'll leave you to your browsing."

Tyler smiled, trying to put her at ease. No doubt she'd heard that he devoured local maidens for breakfast, and the truth was that, oh, yes, he would love to lean close for a quick taste of those full, innocent, berry-tinted lips. But if he tried to kiss Lilah Austin, he'd be no better than the jerk who'd just left the store. Worse, actually, since he was a virtual stranger, not a friend like her "John." Besides, as a rule he didn't associate with the kind of women who inhabited Sloane's Cove. He might play hard and fast where women were concerned, but he had a hint of a conscience. He made sure the females he took to his bed had the same no-ties attitude toward commitment as himself, and he knew better than to get involved with women who expected a man to be more than just a passing friend or a brief source of physical pleasure.

"I'm finding everything I need, Ms. Austin," he finally said, gentling his voice to put her at ease. "But thank you for the offer. You have a very fine store. An impressive collection of local history."

"It's my specialty," she conceded. "My passion, actually, so I guess it's a good thing I own a bookstore. It helps me support my truly bad habit of buying every book there is on the history of Maine. I just can't seem to resist the temptation."

He chuckled. "A vice, Ms. Austin?"

She shrugged. "I guess we all have them. That is, most of us do. Most normal people, that is. We—well, we just wouldn't be human without a few…weaknesses, would we?"

Her attempt to backpedal, and that luscious blush that kissed her pale throat, told Tyler that rumors of his own weaknesses had traveled through town. He was known to be a man of appetites, a man who indulged his desires.

"I guess we wouldn't," he said, not bothering to keep the amusement from his eyes. "Thank you for your help, Ms. Austin." He tilted his head, preparing to take his leave. Interesting about her knowledge of local history. He could use some assistance on this project he was working on. He wondered if she might be of help, but that would mean close contact with Lilah Austin. Might not be wise. For his own reasons he preferred not to get too involved with the people of Sloane's Cove, and where this lovely woman was concerned, he wasn't absolutely sure he could be trusted not to break his own unwritten rules, and trespass. When she'd said the word *passion,* a few seconds ago, a jolt of awareness had gone through him. He'd had a rough desire to hear her whispering to him fervently in the dark, telling him what he could do to give her pleasure. No doubt he'd been working too hard, playing too little lately, and for a man who made a habit of always making time for plenty of play, that was a dangerous omission. It would be better not to test his self-control by spending too much time with a woman whose very voice made him think of tangling his limbs with hers. No doubt he could find someone else to help him unearth the secrets of Sea Watch, his mother's former home, if the answers he was seeking continued to elude him.

But his thoughts were put on hold as a young woman rushed up to Lilah.

''Lilah,'' the girl was saying, bringing her hands to her face. ''Is it true? Everyone's talking about it. Did John Claxton really just propose marriage?''

Lilah took a deep breath. She gave the tiniest embarrassed shrug, and Tyler said goodbye, excused himself and began to edge away. ''It's been a long day, Natalie. Could we talk later?'' he heard Lilah say.

The other woman sighed. ''You never were any good at dodging an issue, Lilah. He did, didn't he? Oh, my goodness, that's three men who've proposed to you in less than two weeks. What's going on, Lilah?''

Tyler had his back turned, but he could almost feel Lilah Austin blushing again. He wondered if that pretty color warmed her skin and what her flesh would feel like pressed against a man's cooler touch. The lady had received three proposals in two weeks? Intriguing.

"Nothing's going on, Natalie," Lilah said, a bit too emphatically. Her voice was so laced with feeling that Tyler couldn't help but turn and look at her. "Nothing," she said, more calmly. "And everything. Oh, what do you think's going on, Natalie? Since my sister got married last month, I'm the last single Austin, and my brothers have turned their attention to me. They want their baby sister married, tied down and taken care of, and they want it done their way. They're sending men over here to hit on me and wear down my self-control. It's to the point where I'm beginning to be suspicious of every single man who steps in the door to buy a book."

She looked away from her friend's face then and ended up staring right into Tyler's eyes.

Her own eyes widened.

Tyler couldn't help it. He was grinning.

"Well, I didn't mean you," she said. "Of course I didn't mean you. You're Tyler Westlake."

Something sharp shifted deep within Tyler's soul. He should have been used to such comments. All of the Westlakes were notorious when it came to the relationship game. Marriage-minded women from strict backgrounds steered clear or risked being pulled into the Westlake marriage machine where mates were taken, bedded and discarded at an alarming rate. Of course, she wouldn't know that Tyler didn't play that game. The marriage mill had ended with him as far as he was concerned. He'd allowed himself one marriage, it had failed, and he refused to fall into the family pattern. Westlakes were notoriously bad at everything that came after the wedding. Binding partnerships were now a dead issue for him.

"No offense taken, Ms. Austin," he said with a tilt

of his head. ''Besides, you're safe with me. You'd be an absolutely beautiful bride, but like you I'm not interested in marriage. If any more potential grooms come your way in the next few minutes, though, feel free to shake the shelves or give me a whistle. I'll just be one aisle away. Call on me if you need me.''

Her eyes widened still more, and then she chuckled. ''I might just do that, Mr. Westlake. It's good to know that there's still one man my brothers can't coerce into proposing to me. Are you sure you don't want that book on crocheting lace doilies?''

''Maybe some other time,'' he said, trying not to laugh at her friend's openmouthed, confused expression. ''Not much time for crocheting lace doilies these days. I'll stick to history for now.''

He turned away.

''Mr. Westlake?'' a soft voice called when he had barely gone three steps.

He turned and looked over his shoulder.

''Thank you,'' Lilah said slowly. ''You were…very nice to me. I appreciate the rescue. If there's ever anything I can do for you…''

For just an instant he heard a woman's soft voice offering him something he definitely wanted to take. But like lightning, the sizzle had passed almost before the thought could form. Tyler realized that those blue eyes were, indeed, absolutely innocent. Those lovely lips weren't for the likes of him. She had been a young, sweet girl when he'd seen her last, and now she was a young, sweet woman. She wanted to offer him a tangible reward as thanks for his generosity, when the truth was that he'd taken more from women than he'd ever given.

He shook his head. ''Your young man would have left on his own in time.''

Suddenly leaving seemed like a darn good idea. Being strong and decent enough to stay away from Lilah Austin's part of town these next few weeks seemed like an even better one.

''Go find some less virginal lips to plunder, Westlake,'' he whispered beneath his breath as he left the store a few minutes later.

Good advice. He hoped he'd take it.

When the phone rang later that night, Lilah was lying in bed going through a book distributor's catalog, but her mind was nowhere near where it should be. This business with her brothers was getting out of hand. She'd known that even before Tyler Westlake had rounded the corner in her bookshop, taken one look at the picture she and John must have made and raised that slightly mocking eyebrow.

She could feel herself blushing even now.

Of course, Tyler had always been able to make her blush, even when she'd been eleven years old to his fourteen. He'd only spent a few summers here in Sloane's Cove, Maine, but all the girls in town had been giggly in his presence. All but her. Tyler, with his thick dark hair and lazy green eyes had made her heart beat faster, just as he had every other girl, but she'd been too shy and tongue-tied to even squeak, much less giggle when he passed by. Once, he found her gazing dreamily at his house, like a Juliet waiting for her Romeo. She'd thought she would die on the spot or possibly blush to death. As it was, she tried to stammer that she had to go home, but had ended up merely fleeing. After that day, all he had to do was glance her way and she colored up, and the worst thing was that her embarrassing propensity for blushing seemed to amuse him. He always grinned at her, which only made things worse. She had an awful habit of being awkward and stumbling when she got embarrassed.

No doubt Tyler thought she was probably running into walls right this minute, still a mess at twenty-eight.

Lilah smiled and tossed the catalog aside. She *had* very nearly walked into the door when she'd come home tonight, but that had simply been her preoccupation with her brother problem. She didn't do much bumping into walls these days. Mostly she spent her time quietly, when she wasn't trying to hide from the men her brothers sent by.

"What were you thinking, Hank?" she whispered.

She was definitely going to have to talk to her brothers. Again.

As if her thoughts had triggered something, the phone rang.

Lilah groaned. Her hand hovered near the receiver.

"Please don't let it be John Claxton or some other man looking for a good, quiet wife who won't cause him any trouble," she muttered as she curled her fingers around the white plastic handset.

For half a second Tyler's face floated in her imagination, but she quickly dismissed that thought. The man had simply come into her store looking for a book. Rumor had it that Tyler was going to restore his mother's old home and turn it into one of his award-winning historical-theme restaurants. Another rumor had him holding midnight orgies with all the women who'd arrived for their vacations after hearing that one of America's wealthiest bachelors would be sunning in Sloane's Cove on Mt. Desert Island these next few weeks.

Lilah frowned. There were certainly plenty of women in Sloane's Cove these days casting provocative looks Tyler's way. She wondered how many would get lucky and snag his attention while he was here. Tyler might be here for work, but he was not the kind of man to be without a woman in his bed for long.

The phone rang for the eighth time. She had an answering machine, but she only used it when she was away. After all, this was Sloane's Cove. Everyone knew her, they knew she was home. It seemed wrong somehow to ignore the telephone or to screen her calls. The only reasons for not answering the phone were embarrassing ones. So, on the next ring, she lifted the receiver with a clatter of plastic against plastic.

"Hello," she said suddenly, in a clipped and overly loud voice.

"Whoa, Lilah. Don't worry. I'm not calling to propose to you," a female voice laced with laughter said. "But if that's the tone of voice you used when you turned down John today, I'm surprised the man is still standing and that his blond hair isn't singed black. Shot him right through the heart, did you?"

Lilah rolled her eyes and smiled at her twin's voice. "You know very well that John's heart wasn't in any way connected to his proposal, Helena. He was just looking for a well-behaved, easy-to-train woman and a good baby-sitter."

"Umm. If that's what he told you, then I don't wonder you threw him out on the street, but I'm not exactly buying into that. Have you seen your face when you're working in your bookstore, Lilah? You get this sort of…I don't know, dreamy orgasmic expression.''

Lilah chuckled. ''Okay, maybe I do get a bit carried away with my lust for the written word, but believe me, John wasn't pushing any of my romantic buttons today, nor was he trying to. I don't think our brothers have any desire to send me a man that could make me even mildly orgasmic. In fact, they'd no doubt pound on any man who so much as suggested he ever had any desire to look lower than my eyeballs. They simply want me married and cared for by a man who isn't going to rock anyone's boat, including my own. I'm sure they list all my most practical, boring assets when they talk me up to the local males. I tell you, Helena, it's maddening being managed this way.''

''Makes you feel a little crazy, doesn't it? A little wild? Like you want to do something outrageous to show them that you're a full-grown woman, doesn't it?''

''That's it exactly,'' Lilah said with a long sigh of frustration. She remembered how only a few weeks ago, when Helena had been pregnant and unmarried, the Austin brothers had made her their special project. At least until she'd found her own man.

''So, what can I do to stop them?'' Lilah asked. ''This could go on for weeks. Even in a town this size, there are lots of men who fit the Austin males' definition of staid husband material. Especially in the summer when the island is swollen with tourists.''

The silence on the other end of the line went on too long. ''Be strong,'' Helena finally said. ''Be Lilah—all you want to be and only what you want to be. The boys love you and they want you to be happy, but you've always been so…''

''Spineless,'' Lilah offered.

''Good,'' Helena countered. ''You've been good. You always go along with whatever you think will make the other person happy, but, Lilah, this is *your* happiness we're talking about now. Only you know what's right for you. If it's not marriage, don't let them push you into it.''

''I won't. That's not going to happen, but…''

''But what, sweetie?''

''I do want to marry someday, Helena, but I just want to find my own husband, in my own time. And frankly, it's very tough to even breathe these days. I have the feeling that every man who looks at me is seeing me through our brothers' eyes.''

''Now there's a sobering thought. Why don't you just tattoo the word *docile virgin* across your forehead and save everyone the trouble of talking to the Austin brothers?''

''There's a thought,'' Lilah mused.

''I was kidding.''

''I know.''

''I'm worried about you, Lilah. You're too good for your own good. Makes me want to hit someone. Really hard, too. Jackson had to restrain me to keep me from driving over to John Claxton's house and kicking him for embarrassing you publicly today.''

Lilah felt her eyes begin to mist. She and Helena were as different as twins could be personalitywise, but they loved each other fiercely, and Helena was the only one who really knew her from the inside out. Her sister had been ecstatically happy these past few weeks. Lilah wanted her to stay that way.

"Thanks, Helena, but don't worry, sweetie. I'm going to take care of this. I can do it once I figure the thing out. In the meantime I'll just have to make the pigheaded Austin males realize that while I love them to pieces, I'm not going to let them treat me like a child."

"What are you going to do?"

"I don't know yet, but I have the feeling that when I decide, it's going to be something very un-Lilah-like. Something drastic. Maybe even something—I don't know—something exciting," she told her sister as they ended their conversation.

But the conversation lingered in Lilah's thoughts. The word *exciting* had conjured up a vision of Tyler Westlake with his dark as midnight hair and his lie-back-and-make-love-to-me-sweetheart voice. She almost gasped, the vision was so strong, so vibratingly real. Now, there was a man who was the exact opposite of everything her brothers were looking for in a husband for her. It would certainly shock them if she ended up married to a man like that.

Not that she ever would.

The trouble was that the type of man she was looking for was dangerously close to her brothers' ideal. She wanted a good man, a family man. She just wanted him to want her for the woman she was deep inside because he loved her, not because she was quiet and not likely to cause him any trouble.

For once, she would *like* to cause a man trouble. She wished she could make a man lose sleep. It would be a welcome change to have a man feel about her the way women felt about Tyler.

Maybe she should have asked him for some pointers before he left her store today.

On that crazy, preposterous thought, Lilah smiled and snuggled under the covers.

Tyler Westlake giving her lessons in how to attract the opposite sex.

What could be more unlikely?

Chapter Two

As Lilah strolled into town early the next morning, a disturbing sight greeted her. The quaint seaside shops all looked the same, stately and slightly weathered. The tang of the sea air was no different than usual. But Kyle Hayward was leaning against the light pole outside her shop. Kyle, who was very nice, very old-fashioned, who had always felt that her sister, Helena, was too wild to be womanly. Since it was too early for Kyle to be looking for a book, Lilah had a bad feeling about his presence, but it wasn't just Kyle who was making her feel so ruffled, she realized.

In the park at the end of the street, Tyler was seated on the back of a bench, his white shirtsleeves rolled to his elbows, the wind teasing his dark, handsome hair, a book opened in his hands. Miriam Dunworth, who owned the town's most luscious bosom, was on the seat bench, gazing up at him worshipfully. The woman picked up a book and held it out to Tyler the way a woman might offer a man wine…or her lips.

To Lilah's knowledge, Miriam had not cracked a book since she turned in her prom queen tiara and graduated from high school, but the rumor was out on the streets: Natalie had read it in the latest edition of the tabloids and had called Lilah at the crack of dawn to tell her the news. Tyler *was* planning to restore his mother's mansion. He was going to wave his magic wand and turn Sea Watch into an exclusive restaurant, rife with historical detail. To do that he needed information, historical records, the written word. He would no doubt be very grateful to whoever supplied him with what he was looking for, and so Lilah suspected that Miriam was about to have an epiphany, to discover that the written word was very sexy.

As she watched them, Tyler turned his head and looked directly into Lilah's eyes. A small smile lifted the corners of his lips. Then he took one look at Kyle, who was clearly watching Lilah, waiting for her, and Tyler tilted his head. A question. Did she need his help?

How embarrassing, even if it was gratifying to think he would leave Miriam's side to help her.

Quickly Lilah shook her head. She took a deep breath, preparing to greet Kyle.

Kyle smiled as she neared him. He had a nice smile. She remembered that he'd always been a nice person. They'd played together as children.

"Good morning, Lilah," he said, straightening to walk toward her. "I was wondering if you'd have lunch with me."

Lilah blinked. It was only seven-thirty in the morning.

He smiled at her confusion. "Thomas said that once

you were in your store, a man would be lucky to entice you out before closing time. I thought I should catch you before then.''

Oh, Thomas, she thought, with a trace of disappointment. Thomas was the youngest of the four Austin brothers. He'd often been her ally when they were younger. Now he was worrying about her, too. The truth was that there was nothing wrong with having lunch with Kyle. He was a nice man, but saying yes would only fuel her brothers' efforts. They would think she was weakening.

She smiled back. ''Thank you, Kyle, but I usually just have lunch in my office.''

''You could do something different today.'' He took a step closer. There was a profound look of determination on his face. Lilah remembered that Kyle had been engaged just a few months earlier, only something had gone wrong and he was free again. Free but not completely recovered, she suspected.

''I...'' She didn't know what to say. She didn't know the particulars of his situation, and she didn't want to wound him, but she had a terrible feeling that saying yes would only prolong the inevitable. Would it be so wrong to just have a sandwich with the man? Maybe he needed someone to talk to.

''I thought maybe you and I could get to know each other better,'' he said suddenly. ''I know I was wild in my younger days.'' He had been. He'd dated Miriam, Lilah remembered. ''But when a man gets older, he wants someone more...quiet, more calm, more—''

No trouble and easy to manage. The thought slipped in.

''Kyle,'' she said gently. ''What did Thomas say to you?''

His ears turned slightly rosy. ''Just that your business seemed to have settled in now and you'd probably be looking to the future. You know?''

She knew. Thomas had told Kyle that she was probably ready to start looking for a husband.

A giggle drifted to them and both Lilah and Kyle turned toward where Miriam was laughing up at Tyler.

A low growl came from Kyle's throat. ''She should be ashamed, flaunting herself that way.''

Lilah glanced at Kyle who was looking a bit too angry. She wondered if there wasn't more to Kyle's offer of lunch than she had suspected, if there wasn't a little bit of jealousy involved, a little bit of ''I'll show you, Miriam,'' and she suddenly felt very tired.

Tyler looked up then. He glanced at Kyle, who was no doubt looking like a cherry bomb whose fuse had already been lit. With a pleasant nod to Miriam, he rose from the bench and began to walk toward Lilah, purposefully unrolling his sleeves, buttoning his cuffs. He seemed to grow taller and more commanding with every step.

''Good morning, Lilah,'' he said when he was about six feet away. He swung his head slowly toward Kyle. ''Am I interrupting anything?''

A sweet liquid sense of relief flowed through her. She felt sorry for Kyle, but she didn't have the solution to what was ailing him, and she was sure that having lunch with the man would only complicate matters for both of them.

''I was just about to go inside,'' she said. ''Thank you for the offer, Kyle. Maybe another day?''

He shrugged and began to walk down the street to where Miriam was looking back their way.

Lilah glanced up at Tyler, who was studying her intently. She ducked her head and fumbled in her purse for her key, hoping she wasn't blushing again. It was awful having your emotions so visible to any handsome, passing male. She dismissed the fact that Kyle hadn't made her blush at all. She and Kyle had probably run around in diapers together, after all.

Finally she found the keys—and promptly dropped them. They fell to the sidewalk with a metallic clatter.

Lilah blew out a deep, frustrated sigh. At least she hadn't walked into the wall. She reached down for the keys—and found her fingers colliding with Tyler's. His hand was much larger than hers. His fingers were warm against her own. Sudden, pleasant sensation arced through her fingertips. Lilah went completely still. She tried to concentrate on not letting her humiliating schoolgirl reaction to Tyler's touch show.

Gently Tyler unfolded her hand from the keys.

''Allow me,'' he said, in that deep, low voice that sent tremors dancing through her. ''Your hands are shaking. What did that guy say to disturb you so? He looked like a man intent on bloodletting.''

Lilah looked down at her fingers. They *were* trembling slightly, but she knew it was because Tyler had touched her, because she was flustered by his nearness. She'd already forgotten about Kyle.

A small shaky laugh escaped her. ''I think it was *your* blood—or maybe Miriam's—that Kyle was interested in. He seemed to take exception to seeing the two of you together.''

Tyler raised both brows. To his credit he didn't mention the fact that Kyle had been talking to her while his eyes were shooting daggers at another woman. Lilah was grateful. A woman could take just so much humiliation in a day.

"The woman—Miriam?—was just offering me some research material on the history of the area. A family Bible, I believe, that contained some records of local births and marriages."

Lilah couldn't help laughing at that. She was pretty sure Miriam had meant to offer a lot more than research. She opened the door of her shop. "And Kyle was just inviting me to lunch. It had nothing to do with the fact that my brothers had probably just told him I would make a willing, docile wife."

The cool air of the dark shop filtered outside. Lilah stepped into the shadows. Tyler stepped in right behind her, his body so close she could feel the heat at her back.

"And would you?"

She took a deep, slow breath, inhaling Tyler's warm, male scent.

"Would I what?" she asked faintly.

"Would you make a willing, docile wife?"

She shrugged. "Eventually? Who knows? I've never been a wife."

"And you don't want to be one."

"Not yet."

"I'd say," he said, as she turned to face him and found his body even closer than she'd thought, "that you're not getting your message across. Was that proposal number four?"

"We didn't get that far," she said with a slow shake of her head. "Kyle took one look at you and—"

"He got distracted," Tyler finished for her, "but he would have asked you in time."

"I certainly wouldn't be that presumptuous."

Tyler's eyes glowed with amusement. "I would. He had that look about him. Let's face it, Lilah. It's mating season in Sloane's Cove, and you're the woman that every man wants."

The store suddenly seemed overly warm, the walls were too close. It occurred to Lilah that anyone could walk in at any minute. It also occurred to her that she might not care. But she had always cared about appearances. Appearances were good to hide behind. They kept a woman safe.

She took a deep breath, reaching for her store-owner persona. "It's not me they want, Tyler," she said calmly, cooler now, "but the woman they think I am."

"What woman is that?"

She lifted one shoulder in dismissal. "Oh, I don't know. The good woman that every man wants. The woman who won't make any waves, cause any upheaval in a man's life."

"That's what every man wants?"

"No, I suppose that's an overstatement, an oversimplification, but there are plenty who do. Especially men who've gone over a bumpy road with another woman recently."

Tyler nodded. He lounged against the wall, filling up the tiny space of her store's entrance. "And what kind of woman are you, really?"

She raised her chin and stared at him defiantly. "A woman who knows what she wants, a woman who wants a man to choose her for who she really is, not because he simply wants an uncomplicated existence.

I do want a husband someday, Tyler, but the right husband.''

''Your brothers know this?''

''My brothers are brothers. They want to protect me, to keep me safe, to ensure my future now.''

''You must be driving them crazy, then.''

He smiled down at her, and she couldn't help but smile back.

''I guess I am, at least a little,'' she admitted. ''And what are you looking for, Tyler? Everyone says you're planning on fixing up Sea Watch, but that you're not going to live there.''

He held out his hands in dismissal. ''Sea Watch was my mother's home, not mine, and I don't think even she was very happy there. Like your young men, she was always looking for something that didn't exist. I suppose that was why she and my father both married so many times. They were always reaching for the unattainable. At any rate, yes, now that she's gone and the property's been turned over to me, I'm going to fix it up and turn it into a restaurant. My youngest stepbrother will be getting married in a month. I'll turn it over to him when it's done. His bride-to-be has a yen for the coast.''

Lilah's eyes widened. ''You're going to do all that work and then simply walk away from it?''

''I know how it sounds, but don't look so alarmed. It's the way I work. I'm the oldest of the Westlakes, but I have plenty of stepbrothers and stepsisters. When my father died, the business was in trouble. The move to specialize and base our restaurants exclusively in areas rich with history paid off. Since then, my siblings and I have worked out a system. I find a suitable building, handle the research, renovation and get things running. Then I move on, and one of them steps in. It works well. Usually. This building is proving to be more of a problem. Many of the records were apparently lost.''

''So you're still looking. Miriam's Bible?'' she said, trying not to smile.

He grinned. ''The lady was very persuasive about wanting to contribute. The Bible, unfortunately, won't be much help.''

Lilah was pretty sure she understood. Miriam's family members were all known to be a bit outlandish. Piety wasn't one of their virtues, and she would bet that diligent record keeping wasn't a family asset, either. Fortunately, Miriam had plenty of other assets including a good heart—and a killer body.

''You need a good researcher,'' she blurted out, blinking away the strangely irritating image of Tyler with Miriam.

''I usually have them, but this one—I thought I'd handle it myself. It is my own home, after all. I suppose I was a bit hesitant about opening up the family skeletons to a stranger.''

Lilah nodded. ''It can be embarrassing having everyone knowing your business.''

For a minute Tyler looked troubled, serious. He reached out and tucked his finger under her chin. ''I won't be telling people that Kyle nearly proposed to you this morning if that's what you're thinking, Lilah. There's no need to worry. It's early. Almost no one was about. No one needs to know anything you don't want them to know.''

His gentle tone, the deep concern in his eyes, sent

Lilah's senses reeling. She knew what Miriam must have been feeling when she gazed up at the man, and for a minute Lilah felt sorry for the other woman. Because she had hoped for what Lilah would never hope for. Lilah knew that Tyler wasn't for any one woman.

But he was so very good at attracting women. Kyle had gotten jealous just looking at the man, even though Tyler had no real apparent interest in Miriam. He'd seen what he wanted to see, what anyone who didn't know Tyler might have thought.

She didn't know Tyler, Lilah reminded herself.

No, but she knew he didn't want a wife. She knew he had a way of making men disappear when they came near her. She knew that he needed some help with his current project.

"Tyler?"

"Yes, Lilah? You're looking worried. I meant what I said, both yesterday and today. Any man gives you grief, you just come find me. And my lips are sealed."

She looked at those lips and wondered how many women he'd slayed with that wonderful, persuasive mouth of his.

"I—" Lilah glanced out the window. She saw her brother Frank heading down the street toward the shop, grim purpose in his expression, and Lilah simply reacted. She shut the door that was still standing open and locked it, pulling down the shade she almost never drew. Then she grabbed Tyler's hand and began tugging him toward her office at the back of the store.

The man was a mountain, though. He didn't move.

"Lilah?"

"Yes?" She let go and glanced up at him, trying not to look worried and doing her best not to think about the fact that she had been attempting to bodily force the man into a small private space with her.

"Is there another man coming to propose to you?"

She shook her head, sending her long locks floating and sifting down around her shoulders. "Worse. My brother."

Tyler chuckled. "Should I get rid of him?"

The urge to say yes was strong. "No, that would be—that would be cowardly of me, wouldn't it?"

"Are you afraid of him?" Sharp anger colored Tyler's voice. He turned as if he was going to confront Frank.

Lilah grabbed for his hand again.

He stopped and looked at her, a gentle question in his eyes. "I'm not afraid," she explained. "I'm just…tired. They mean well, all my brothers do. They just don't understand. They've always pushed hard to get the things they wanted. They see me as a woman who sits and waits, and that scares them. They're afraid I'll still be waiting in ten years if they don't do something."

"I'll explain it to them." He turned again, and she clutched his sleeve. The strength of the muscles beneath his clothing sent Lilah a message. He intended to protect her from whoever dared to force anything on her.

"Tyler?"

He turned. Waited.

"Why?"

He stared deep into her eyes. "I have some experience with people forcing their will on others. Personal experience. It's never sat well with me."

She was both touched and angry. Someone had

taught him that lesson, and now he was prepared to go to battle for her. Because she wasn't battling hard enough for herself.

Sudden determination and conviction rolled through her.

''Maybe if I took more control of my life, made some real changes, they'd stop trying so hard,'' she said. ''I...I could use your help,'' she said suddenly.

''I'll explain to them so that they'll understand,'' he agreed. ''I'm used to negotiating with people who don't always see things from all angles. Don't worry,'' he said.

She smiled then. ''Tyler, I'm sure you're an expert at what you do. You obviously have the track record to prove it, but these are my brothers. They'll only believe what they see with their eyes.''

''You're not suggesting that I put my fist in your brother's face?'' He narrowed his eyes in mock disbelief. ''How bloodthirsty you've become over the years, Lilah.''

His voice was so very sensual, so very suggestive, Lilah wondered if she wasn't completely insane for even thinking what she was thinking, but then, she'd been worried for some time about the way events were unfolding in her life. Tyler looked like an answer to a prayer.

''I don't want you to hit my brother, Tyler,'' she said with a small shake of her head that sent her hair cascading about her. ''I want you to let him think that you're—''

She felt the heat rising in her face.

''Lilah?''

She looked away, felt his thumb brush gently over her hot skin.

''You want him to think I'm what?'' he coaxed, in a tone that could have made any woman do anything. If he'd asked her to unzip her skirt and let it fall to the floor right that minute, she just might have done it, Lilah thought, as the blood pounded through her body.

''I want you to—would you mind letting my brother think you're…interested in me?'' Her breath came out on a choked whisper, and she tried to clear her throat. ''That is, part of the reason my brothers aren't giving me any breathing space is because they think I'm just sitting here gathering dust, that I'm not even dating,'' she explained in a hot rush. ''They're right, but right now, I'm afraid to even smile at most men for fear they'll think I'm encouraging a proposal. But you… you wouldn't think that. You know that I'm not looking right now. So, if you could just smile at me a little, maybe even go to lunch or to dinner with me, it would make my brothers take a step or two back. I think. I wouldn't expect you to do this for free, either. I'd want to give you something in return.''

He was grinning at her, almost laughing, really.

''What?'' she said. ''Do you think it's totally hopeless, that no one would even begin to think that you could be interested in me? I know I'm not built like Miriam and that I'm not exactly the kind of woman you usually date, but—''

His warm fingers brushed her lips, stopping her speech as a slow pounding sounded on the door.

''I think that I've never heard you make such a long speech, my quiet little bookseller,'' he whispered in her ear, leaning close so that her brother couldn't hear him, his lips nearly touching her skin, his breath warming her.

A slow shiver of unfamiliar need arced through her, and Lilah faltered. She had absolutely no experience at this kind of thing, and, looking up into those woman-slayer green eyes, she wondered if she'd completely lost her senses. Undoubtedly she had. She didn't do these kind of impetuous, crazy things. Who would believe this farce? Why would he help her?

"I can make it worth your while. I can help you find all the information you need to open your restaurant in time," she promised.

"That would be very nice," he said, "but we'll talk about it more later. Right now your brother is planning on calling a locksmith. Perhaps you should let him in."

Lilah nodded. She started to step forward.

"Lilah, wait."

She turned and looked into Tyler's eyes. "If we're going to do this, love, let's do it right," he said.

And with one swift move he unfastened the top two buttons of her modest blouse, exposing a good two inches of skin. He reached up and loosened his tie, pulling it to the side and yanking open the top button of his own shirt.

"Tyler?" Her voice quivered slightly.

"Shh, angel. Be still. I won't hurt you." But he took her in his arms and lowered his lips to hers. Her breath froze in her throat as the sensation of being expertly kissed by Tyler Westlake hit her. His hands were in her hair, his mouth was moving over hers, slowly, so very slowly, dragging an instant response from her, igniting nerve endings she hadn't even been aware of. A low whimper escaped her as Tyler continued to plunder her lips. Sensation was exploding within her, making her ache, making her cling. She reached up and slid her fingers into his hair and held on.

When he released her, she knew that she was looking a little dazed. Her lips felt as if they belonged to another woman, her lipstick was no doubt smudged, her hair no longer neatly combed.

She gazed up at Tyler, who was studying her from beneath fierce, hooded eyes.

''Go let your brother in, angel,'' he finally said in a low, raspy voice, ''and tell him that if he has any men to send round this evening, that he's wasting his time. You're already taken tonight.''

Chapter Three

The doorbell rang that evening, and Lilah swallowed hard before going to answer it, but it wasn't Tyler as she'd expected. Her four brothers stood on her doorstep, muscled arms folded against their chests, frowns firmly planted on their handsome faces.

"Hi, shrimp," her oldest brother, Bill, said, leaning to kiss her cheek and then step past her into the house. "We just thought we'd come by and invite you over to a family gathering tonight at my house. Genevieve's making her famous roast chicken."

Lilah glanced up at Frank, who had the good grace to look slightly sheepish as he filed in at the end of the line of brothers.

"That's very nice of you, Bill," Lilah said, closing the door behind her, "and very nice of Genevieve, but I'm afraid I've already made plans. I would have thought Frank might have mentioned that fact."

"He might have," Hank agreed. "And that might be the reason for the family meeting."

"Helena, too?" Lilah asked.

Thomas scowled. "Helena said she'd be there if you were, but she wasn't betting on you showing up."

Lilah smiled. Leave it to her twin to know the way things were.

"We'll do it another night," she said soothingly.

Hank snorted. "Another night will be too late. You can't go out with that guy, Lilah. He's bad news for a woman like you."

Lilah stiffened and raised her chin. "And...I would be exactly what kind of woman, Hank?"

Her most stubborn brother met her head to head. He frowned down at her with those lovely hazel eyes that had once made women swoon before Annette had won his heart. "You're a woman who deserves a good, stable man."

Lilah crossed her own arms. "Someone like John Claxton?" she admonished. "Some man to explain just how grateful I should be that he noticed me?"

Hank took a deep breath and rubbed his jaw. "John might have been a mistake, I'll admit."

"And Kyle, who obviously is looking for a woman to try to make Miriam jealous?"

Thomas shifted from one foot to the other, looking like an errant schoolboy, in spite of his football player physique. "The guy never told me about Miriam," he explained helplessly.

Bill held up one hand. "We just want you to be happy, Lilah. We want you to have everything you deserve. You're alone so much of the time. You hide in that bookstore, then you go straight home and sink into your books there. A woman needs more. *Any* person needs more," he amended, when she started to open her mouth in protest.

What could she say? She knew they were interfering in her life because they cared, but—

''I appreciate the fact that you want to help, but I'm a grown-up, guys,'' she said.

''You still have fairy tales on your shelves,'' Frank said, his eyes roaming over the books that were everywhere in sight.

Lilah blew out a big breath. ''That doesn't mean I believe in them anymore, Frank.''

He crossed his arms again. ''Well, you should. You should have everything you want, and I—*we're*—just concerned about you. We want you to have the golden ball, babe, the whole thing. A guy who thinks you make the sun rise every morning, someone who'll give you babies and make you want to close the pages of your books now and then.''

Lilah felt her eyes misting. The truth was that she wanted the life Frank described, but how could she explain to her brother that it just wasn't the kind of thing that a person could force? It was the kind of thing a woman wanted to achieve on her own. The fact that it hadn't happened yet and, yes, that it didn't look like it might ever happen, didn't make a difference.

''You don't even date all that often,'' Bill said angrily.

''I do,'' she insisted. ''Sometimes.''

''When?''

Lilah felt her color rising. She had to think back a long way to her last dating disaster, and she really didn't want to think about it at all. ''I went to the movies with Edison Samuels.''

Her brothers exchanged ''the look.''

''That guy,'' Thomas declared, ''gives bottom feeders a good name.''

Lilah refrained from commenting. Although she would never go that far, she had to admit that Edison had hurt her feelings pretty badly. He'd hung around her store for weeks, professed an interest in her, then at the end of their "date," she'd discovered the real reason for his attachment: he was thinking of writing a book. He thought she might have some useful "connections."

"I was just making a point," she said.

"And what kind of point are you making with Tyler Westlake?" Bill asked. "He's not your type, either. I've heard plenty of stories about the man that would send you running in the opposite direction."

"Don't say another word, Bill," Lilah said. She'd heard plenty of stories about Tyler, too, but the truth was that he'd come to her rescue twice now. Her brothers couldn't know that Tyler's interest in her lay only in the research department, but she knew. Everything between the two of them was clear and up-front, and she wouldn't allow her brothers to throw stones.

The sound of a car driving down the road snagged everyone's attention.

Thomas stepped forward. "Look, Lilah, we may have botched a few things these past weeks, but we intend to be more careful in the future. There are plenty of men in Sloane's Cove who'd be good, caring husbands. If you'd only try out a few. It wouldn't hurt to date a man who's looking for a stable relationship."

"That wouldn't be Tyler Westlake, in case you hadn't heard," Hank said, as the noise of the car's engine died away. "The Westlakes aren't known for relationships that last more than a minute, even when there's marriage involved. The man's already gotten started on his succession of wives."

In spite of her love for her brother, in spite of the fact that she knew what he was saying was true, a protest rose up from deep within Lilah. It was wrong to discuss Tyler this way.

"The Westlakes' private affairs aren't really any of our business, are they?" she asked quietly.

"I hope not," Thomas said.

But at that moment Bill looked out the window he was standing next to. "Look at that, would you? The man drives a silver Maserati. Not exactly a family car, Lilah."

"A Maserati?" Frank said, hastening toward the window. "Get out." His voice was filled with awe.

Lilah did her best to hide her smile, but it was just too difficult.

"Lucky me," she said. "I'll let you guys know how it rides." She began walking to the door.

"You're not leaving, Lilah?" Thomas asked.

"Oh, it's okay, Tom. Just make yourselves at home. There's food in the fridge. It's all right if you stay. Just don't wait up for me. Oh, and call your wives. They'll worry if you don't come home."

Lilah waggled her fingers at her brothers and turned to go.

Bill gave a low chuckle. "Nice try, Lilah, but no. As your stand-in parents, we'll want to meet your date."

"When I was young and Mom and Dad died, you were the best substitute parents Helena and I could have hoped for, but…I'm twenty-eight, big brother."

"Even if you were fifty-eight," he said.

So it was with a sigh and great misgiving that Lilah swung the door open.

Tyler looked down into her eyes, then glanced to the four big males standing behind her.

A slow smile formed on his lips.

"Well, hello there," he said calmly. "Frank, good to see you again so soon. You live here, do you?"

Frank shifted from foot to foot. "Lilah lives alone."

Hank shoved his elbow into his brother's ribs, making Frank cough. "We're around a lot, though," Hank said.

Tyler tilted his head. "That's good to know. I won't worry about Lilah, then, when I'm not with her. With so many men bothering her lately, it makes a man toss and turn at night."

He gazed down at Lilah, reaching out to gently brush a strand of hair away from her cheek, and she nearly lost her breath. His fingertips dragging against her skin made her want to lean into his touch. The look he was giving her was one of utter possessiveness. She wondered where he'd learned to do that, to put on a show this way—and how many women's hearts that heated expression had melted.

"No need for you to worry," Bill said, muscling forward. "That's what we're here for."

"Glad to hear it. I'm here to steal Lilah away for a while." He held out his hand to her. "Are you… ready?"

For a short second, or maybe ten, her brain stuttered. Was she ready? Ready for their made-up date? Ready for him to kiss her crazy again? Ready to take him into her bed and take his body into hers?

Sucking in a deep, backbone-firming breath of air, she nodded tightly and held out her hand. "Let's do it," she agreed, trying to ignore the way he smiled slightly at her ill-chosen words.

Frank stepped forward and between them as if he would stop them from leaving, and Tyler met his stare.

"Frank," Lilah began softly, but Tyler shook his head.

"He's your brother, Lilah, and he cares what happens to you. That's not a problem for me, Austin," he said. "But if it means you doubt your sister's ability to handle herself or that you don't trust her, then you're out of line. She handled those last two idiots admirably. I might remind you that no matter what you think of me, Lilah has proven herself to be a woman of strength and integrity."

"Never said she wasn't," Frank said, standing his ground.

"Good. I'm glad we're agreed on that point, gentlemen. I wouldn't want to think you were insulting the lady." Tyler's voice was cool, slightly terse, with an air of command that Lilah was sure had served him well in the tough business world where he lived out his days. "Now, if you'll excuse us..." He reached around Frank and folded Lilah's hand into his own.

Frank stood staring for a few seconds more. Then he stepped back. What, after all, was he going to do, short of trying to take Tyler down and locking her in her room? Lilah wondered.

There followed a general shuffling and grumbling by her brothers, but Tyler whisked her away and tucked her into his car.

They were several miles down the road when she finally turned to him.

"I'm sorry about that."

His lips were tilted in a quirky half smile when he turned to her. "Sorry for what? For having brothers who care what happens to you? Don't be."

''I'm not, most of the time, but there are times… well, let's just say I doubt that's what you usually go through when you arrive at a woman's house.''

Tyler smiled and shook his head. No, that wasn't what usually happened. Most of the women he… visited showed up at the door alone and wearing something satin and skimpy. Lilah was wearing a pale-blue sundress that fell below her knees and was topped by a short-sleeved bolero jacket that covered the cream of her shoulders. It was a dress made for an innocent, and there was a definite wholesomeness that emanated from the lady. Not at all like the women he chose to date, but then this wasn't really a date. So why was he going crazy imagining what he would find if he unfastened all those buttons running down the front of her dress?

Don't even try, he ordered himself. No point in torturing himself needlessly when he wasn't about to touch an innocent, and besides, his silence was making the lady uncomfortable. She had grasped the lapels of her bolero and was playing with the fabric, causing it to part ever so slightly. The fact that she was fully covered underneath only made the movement more tantalizing.

And the fact that he was thinking such thoughts only made him a total jerk under the circumstances. He dragged his gaze back to the road.

''Don't worry about what happened at the house. Meeting your brothers was invigorating,'' he said.

Lilah tossed back her hair as a low laugh escaped her.

''I'm sure it was invigorating for my brothers, as well. They're not used to having anyone tell them that they're out of line. Other than Helena, that is.''

''Helena?''

''My twin.''

''Oh, yes, I remember—a bit. A bundle of energy and a flurry of words. Very refreshing.''

When he looked at her again, deep dimples dented her cheeks. ''Helena would love that. Usually people simply call her overwhelming.''

''And what do they call you?''

Lilah's expression turned serious and slightly tense. ''Oh, I don't know,'' she said, holding out one hand. ''Quiet. Serious. Dependable. A bookworm.''

''Sounds terrible,'' he teased.

She wrinkled her nose at him. ''Of course it's not, and I am all those things. It's just that I—well, heavens, I sound so positively boring. Like oatmeal without the brown sugar.''

''Don't knock it. Those guys who have been coming round must have a real taste for oatmeal without brown sugar.''

''They just think I'm safe.''

''And you're not?''

''Okay, you've got me. I *am* safe. I just don't want that to be the most attractive part of me.''

Tyler could have told her that she had many other very attractive and incredibly distracting parts, but that was definitely not a ''safe'' direction to take.

''I guess that's why I asked you to help me this afternoon,'' she offered. ''I wanted to make a point, that I intend to be chosen for more than just convenience, and that I want to have a hand in the choosing. Thank you for helping. You...you can take me home now. I'm pretty sure my brothers have gone home to their wives.''

That was just what he should do—take the lady

home. But Tyler wasn't so convinced that all of her brothers would have left. If he had a sister who looked like Lilah, with Lilah's good nature, what would he do if she walked out of the house with a man who slipped from woman to woman on far too regular a basis? Tyler frowned, reminding himself once more that while he hadn't married over and over again the way his parents had, he was just on a different version of the same treadmill. He wasn't built for steady relationships. The closeness didn't suit him, and his habits were well-known. If he were one of her brothers, he wouldn't be happy with tonight's events—at all. They'd be waiting up for her for sure. She wouldn't have any peace. He turned to look at Lilah.

"Really, it's all right, I'm sure," she said.

He shook his head slowly. "I was sure we had a date."

She looked up at him with those blue, blue eyes. He forced himself to turn his attention back to the road. "You know this wasn't a real date," she accused. "You're just being nice."

He had to smile at that. Very few people ever accused him of being nice. Keeping a cool distance from people had served him well, both in business and in his personal life. He ought to be distancing himself from Lilah right now, too, since this was a nowhere-to-go kind of relationship.

"You have other plans?" he asked.

She hesitated. "No, not tonight."

"Then where would you like to go?"

She thought for a minute, then shifted in her seat. "I'd like to go to your house. Just to see it," she added quickly. "You indicated that you're going to be doing some work on it, that you're interested in the history, and that you're going to make it into a restaurant and turn it over to your brother. This might be my only chance to sneak a peek inside before all the changes take place.''

''Ah, so it's only my house you're interested in, Ms. Austin. Somehow I feel about as boring as oatmeal without the brown sugar.''

Her laugh was deliciously light.

''No one would ever call you boring, Tyler. I'm sure you know that. Mysterious, maybe. Intriguing, definitely. You've kept the people of Sloane's Cove whispering ever since you got here. You've livened up the place. Will you take me?''

Her abrupt change of topic caught him off guard. Would he take her? *Oh, yes,* he thought, followed swiftly by, *Oh, no.* Taking a beautiful innocent like Lilah into his dark and empty home would be decidedly ill-advised. He was only human, after all. A man, and a far-from-perfect one at that. The smart thing would be to simply walk away from this whole situation, this temptation. But the memory of a young, shining-eyed girl gazing at his home with adoration, but too shy to ask to look, too intimidated by his pompous family, stole into his thoughts.

He tried to push the distant memory away. He turned to look at Lilah...and found that her eyes could still speak to him.

''Next stop, Sea Watch,'' he promised, and he turned the car toward the ocean drive.

''You haven't been back here in years,'' she said suddenly. ''Don't you ever miss it?''

He was silent for several minutes, trying to think of the most tactful answer, the one that wouldn't reveal how many painful memories were attached to this place. ‘‘I have lots of homes in lots of cities.’’

‘‘Yes, but Sea Watch is so, well—’’ She shook her head suddenly. ‘‘Obviously, I’m biased. Maine has always been my only home and I love it here. You’re used to a much more exciting life with a greater variety of experiences than one could ever find in Sloane’s Cove.’’

Tyler didn’t answer that. He wasn’t sure he wanted to think about how fast paced and shallow his life must appear to someone like Lilah, especially since it was a life that suited him so very well. It was a life he was suddenly eager to return to.

‘‘So, do you think you’ve made your point to your brothers?’’ he asked, changing the subject.

‘‘You were there. What do you think?’’

He smiled into the growing dark. ‘‘I think leaving you in my hands practically killed them. I’m betting they’re calling up every trustworthy single male friend they have in every town within a hundred miles. Could be many more suitors coming your way in the next few weeks.’’

‘‘I know,’’ she said as he pulled into the circular drive in front of the huge white Georgian with its sweeping side porches, its center gable and its widow’s walk. ‘‘But it was nice to have my own way for one evening, anyway.’’

Her wistful tone caught at his senses, making him long for…something. Tyler felt a tremendous urge to pull her into the circle of his arms and do whatever he could to bring the smile back into her voice.

But he let the feeling drift away, or rather he forced it away. Stupid to allow himself such fanciful thoughts when in a few short weeks he’d be far away and never think of Lilah Austin again. He would be glad that he hadn't done something that had the potential to hurt her in the long run. No doubt those silent urges he was feeling were merely a trick of the night—a combination of the dark, cloud-streaked sky, which still held a fading trace of red, and this building that had housed generations but hadn't really been a home for anyone in forever.

"I love just looking at this place. It's a sanctuary," she said, as he handed her from the car. "Tall and strong and a fitting equal to the wind of the coast, a haven for a man coming home from the sea or the woman waiting for him. I've always thought of it that way. A bit fanciful, I know, and yet..."

"It fits," he agreed.

His voice dropped lower as he stood beside her, gazing at the building, and Lilah looked up at him, trying to gauge what he was thinking. She'd been wondering all afternoon. He wasn't an easy man to read or understand. He hadn't been easy as a boy, either. She hadn't really known him, not well at all. He was so rarely here, and only for a few short weeks every summer. He didn't mingle with the locals when he came, but she remembered a day when she'd thought he might come close enough to become a friend. The summer had been half over. She'd finally gotten up the nerve to smile and say hello without stammering too much when he walked past instead of just blushing at his greeting. He'd smiled back, a smile that had turned his eyes a deeper shade of green and warmed her. They'd somehow fallen into step, tramped along the shoreline paths, scrambling on the rocks and trying to watch for ships in the distance. But the next day he'd simply left. She hadn't seen him since. What must he be thinking now? She couldn't believe she had really asked him to help her escape her brothers' matchmaking schemes, even for a day. It wasn't like her to be so bold, but then, she'd been wanting to step outside her safe barriers, even if just for a day. Why not?

She smiled at that. Why not? Because this was Tyler Westlake she was standing beside, and any woman who got too close to the man risked falling under his spell and coming out of the experience with a bandage holding her heart together.

Any woman but her, of course. She was oatmeal. Very safe.

She smiled up at him.

"What do *you* think when you see your home, Tyler?"

He gazed down at her for long seconds, the night breeze ruffling his dark hair. Then he turned back to the shadowed edges of the building.

"There was a time when I loved this place. I always felt it had stories to tell, stories it had witnessed and was hiding away."

"Absolutely," she said on a whisper. "Sea Watch has seen a great deal of history, the lives and loves of hundreds. Babies being born, generations passing on their wisdom and their follies. What happened?"

"To the house?"

"Why don't you still love Sea Watch?"

He stood silent for a moment, then shrugged as if shaking off something on his shoulder. When he turned to her, the serious side of him had been carefully packed away. He had that wicked grin on his face again, the one that made her heart beat like the wings of a hummingbird flapping hard and fast.

"It's still an interesting building," he admitted. "I

just moved on, grew up. I changed, but the stories... I'm still interested in them. That's the history I'm looking for, not just who built the place and when. The stories at the heart of a building make it come alive. That's what I'm after.''

His voice was like a caress across her skin, teasing her, warming her, making her ache.

''I could help you,'' she said in a sudden whisper. ''I...I know people, places to look.''

He tucked his fingers beneath her chin, urging her to look at him. ''I hope you're not feeling as if you owe me anything for tonight, Lilah. I do what I want to do. I wanted to do this—with you.''

Lilah swallowed hard, searching for her voice, hoping it would not come out too small or squeaky. ''Thank you, and no, I'm not offering out of obligation. I'd...I'd enjoy helping you research your stories. I love that kind of thing. What can I say?'' she asked, trying to smile. ''I'm a research nut.''

''You're a generous woman, but I couldn't just let you do that. This would take time. You're busy with your shop. I would, of course, appreciate any assistance you could offer, but I couldn't do that without repaying you in some way.''

Lilah frowned. ''I don't want money.''

''What *do* you want, Lilah?'' Tyler's words were gentle, but his green gaze seemed to leave no room for her to hide. Lilah felt as if a thunderstorm were about to engulf her, so powerful were her reactions to Tyler's lightest touch, to the way he was studying her.

She lifted her chin, and his hand slid down her skin slightly. What did she want? Her mind jumbled. Right now, with his fingers on her flesh, she wanted Tyler to keep looking at her as if he really wanted her, to keep touching her forever. Men generally didn't look at her that way, and the feelings his mere gaze was calling up made her tremble deep inside.

She wanted more, however. Much more than a touch or a moment or a burning gaze that made her ache—and feel panic because she ached. What she longed for in her dreams was a man who would love her for the woman she was, both on the surface and deep inside where the hidden Lilah lived, a woman who was bold and sensual and strong. That was what she wanted, but neither of those answers was what Tyler was asking her about, and neither of them should be taking up her thoughts right now. Tyler was a temporary neighbor, a man who couldn't supply what she wanted. Still, because he couldn't possibly be her future husband, that made him—well, she guessed that made him ''safe,'' even if it was an odd title to attach to such a man.

''What do I want?'' she said, searching for something light, something that would let both of them off the hook and end this night on a bright, hopeful note. ''I want the chance to research this house, first of all,'' she said truthfully, ''and I want the time to do it. That means I can't be spending my hours evading my brother's plans. You could repay me by giving me a legitimate reason why I can't be available to date my brothers' friends or listen to any more marriage proposals. I want to show my brothers that I'm going to live my life on my terms, and I'm definitely going to find my own husband.''

Tyler slowly slid his hand down her throat, over her shoulder and down to her hand. ''Are you asking me for another date, Lilah?''

''I...I don't know. I hadn't thought. Maybe. I—is that what I just did?''

He swiped one hand over his jaw, and she could see that he was covering a grin. ''Apparently not exactly, since you seem so uncertain. Still, you definitely suggested something that would mean we'd be spending a lot of time together. Do you think that's wise, Lilah? This could create problems for you with your family.''

''And problems for you,'' she admitted.

He studied her with those dark-green eyes of his, and she could swear there was a war going on inside him. ''I'm afraid I already have a problem,'' he finally said. ''One I can't seem to ignore. The problem is that I strongly believe people should be free to follow their dreams. It always bothers me when anyone tries to derail that process. It always has,'' he said, frowning, and Lilah wondered at the flicker of pain she saw in his eyes. Whatever it was, he masked it quickly.

She stared up at him. ''I-I'm sorry. I probably shouldn't have asked you to help me fight my battles. It suddenly seems incredibly selfish and way too impetuous. Crazy talk.''

He shook his head and grinned. ''Not crazy at all, especially since it seems that I'm rather partial to battles. Especially the right kind, which this one is. Besides,'' he said, his voice dropping low, ''you're not just asking me to take up the sword for you. You've offered your expertise. I could use some help,'' he admitted.

She smiled. ''All right. That's good, then. I've been told I can be quite helpful.''

He chuckled, and the sound caught low in his throat. ''It sounds like you've been told a lot of things over the years. Would you be offended if I pointed out that you're being decidedly…unquiet this evening?'' His voice was a low, teasing whisper, and suddenly she wanted to throw her arms around the man and kiss him. The thought should have been funny. After all, what woman didn't want to kiss Tyler?

''Unquiet?'' she said instead. ''I like that. For the next few weeks I don't want to be known as quiet or dependable or safe.''

She stared up at him and shivered as the light breeze drifted across her shoulders.

Immediately he placed his arm around her and began to lead her toward the house and the warmth that lay within.

''What do you want to be known as, Lilah?''

The heat from his body seeped through her skin. His arm was strong, his thigh brushed against hers as they walked. She felt reckless, as if fairy dust were sprinkling from the stars and loosening her tongue.

''I want to be known as a woman to be reckoned with. I want to make men sit up and notice that I have dreams and desires and convictions. I want to be a little bit…I don't know. Dangerous?''

Tyler stopped in his tracks. He turned to face her, framed her face with his hands. A slow smile turned his shadowed features beautifully wicked. ''All right then, Lilah. We'll work together toward our goals. You'll help me dig up the stories I need to bring life to this restaurant and make this gift to my brother extraspecial. I'll help you hold off the army of men trailing you around until you're good and ready to be courted by a man of your own choosing. Together we'll see if we can't bring your dangerous side to the surface.''

''How do we do that?''

He studied her closely for several seconds, his eyes

looking deep into her own. "We find the stories hidden within you, angel, and we…experiment."

He leaned down and covered her lips with his, ever so briefly. A jolt of naked desire pulsed through Lilah. Her breasts felt heavy, her head felt dizzy, even her fingertips tingled. When Tyler took her hand again and led her to his door, she knew she had probably made a tactical error.

This much sensual danger was quite possibly more than she could handle. Tyler was definitely a lot more experienced, more heated, more male than she was used to, and there was absolutely nothing safe about this situation.

A little backpedaling was probably in order right around now. That was what she would normally do. She would be sensible, she would be cautious, regroup. She would admit she'd made a mistake and commit herself to being more careful.

And tomorrow Hank or Bill would present her with another man who would take care of her, but who would never truly know or love the real her.

Lilah swallowed hard. She closed her eyes, stepped through the door and entered Tyler's house.

Chapter Four

This was probably not the wisest thing he'd ever done in his life, Tyler thought late the next afternoon as he pulled up in front of Lilah's cottage in full view of her neighbors. Playing pretend lover to a woman he couldn't actually take to bed was definitely tempting fate. Their tour last night had been short due to lack of light, but today he would be with her for a long while. Smiling at her, possibly touching her.

"Oh, yes, this is not one of your better moves, Westlake," he muttered as she appeared in the window. He got another good glimpse of that willowy body. The slender dress she was wearing was virginal white and fell below her knees. It should have been the safest of garments. He shouldn't have had a sudden vision of her lying on a bed while he slowly slid that long skirt up to bare her thighs, but he did. Fortunately, when Lilah spotted him, she smiled and moved out of his line of vision.

He climbed the three steps leading to her solid,

wooden door and concentrated on remembering that she was doing a favor for him and he was doing a favor in return. This relationship might create the appearance of being built on fire, but it was, in fact, no more than smoke.

"Come in," she said, opening the door and stepping aside to let him pass. "Are you all ready for me?"

"Excuse me?" He raised his brows.

"We were going to plan our strategy today, weren't we?" she asked. "Isn't that why you're here?"

It was. He smiled at her. "Definitely. Let's start by closing the curtains."

At the confused look in her eyes, he slid one hand along her jaw, tipping her chin up. "My car is in your driveway. I'm going to be here for several hours. If we leave the curtains open, any of your neighbors who care to walk by will know we're just talking. If we close them…"

"People will assume we're kissing."

"At the very least."

A dusky blush colored her skin prettily. "Of course. I hadn't thought."

Which was the very reason why he wouldn't touch. It hadn't even occurred to her that a man's first thought on finding her at home alone would be that he was a lucky son of a gun. Or that any man's second thought would be that if he was even more lucky, he could close the door behind him, draw the drapes, strip her clothes from that lovely body and spend the afternoon feasting on her. Deep inside, Lilah Austin was still that shy girl he'd once admired. The fact that she had grown into a lovely, desirable woman who could make a man ache to touch her had apparently been hidden from her.

He wondered why. He meant to do what he could

to help her understand that she had powers she hadn't yet realized.

It was going to be heaven to teach her.

It was going to be pure torture, as well.

Tyler suppressed a groan of frustration and concentrated instead on setting Lilah's mind at ease now that he'd made her uncomfortable. He smiled.

"You wanted to be a bit dangerous, didn't you?"

She took a deep breath. A look of pure determination filled those deep-blue eyes as she firmed her chin and stared resolutely back at him.

"I did. I will be. Where can we start? After we close the curtains, that is?"

She moved to the window and closed one set of white lace curtains. He moved to another and did the same. Shards of daylight filtered in, casting patterns on the golden wood floor.

Lilah, who had been looking slightly shaken up until then, glanced up at him and smiled suddenly. "Lace curtains are probably not the best choice for creating a total look of privacy, are they?"

Tyler shrugged. "Your neighbors won't be able to see much if they're watching."

She rolled her eyes. "Do you think they are?"

"Hmm. Let's see. Single bachelor pays call on lovely single woman who's been collecting proposals by the truckload. What are the odds someone might be curious as to what we're doing in here?"

"Well, Alma Rice lives just a few doors down. She's a good friend and another merchant. Alma also considers herself an expert on what makes a man a man, and she's also the personal bearer of good news regarding the Austin sisters. She'd probably consider this good news. Alma thinks my brothers have been behaving like fussy mother hens.''

Tyler moved closer, close enough so that anyone peeking through the haze of lace curtains would see two silhouettes almost merging.

''So your friend Alma would approve of my being here.''

''The only thing she'd approve of more would be if you were hiding behind *her* lace curtains.''

''It's good to have allies.''

''And a plan. I was wondering if I should try to make myself look more the part.''

He frowned slightly. ''In what way?''

Lilah looked to the side for a second. ''Well, it only seems logical to me that if we're going to convince people that you're at all interested in me, that I should look a bit more like one of your women.''

The term sounded all wrong flowing out of those sweet pink lips. ''My women?''

She nodded resolutely. ''Yes. You know, like the ladies you ordinarily date. Like—'' She glanced around the room, her gaze falling on a stack of magazines.

Quickly she moved to the stack, knelt on the floor and sifted through a few.

''Aha, like this,'' she said, setting one aside and flipping through the pages. There, in the pages of one of New York's society mags, was a color photo of him entering a party with Jillian Sanders. Jillian was a model he had dated briefly last year. She was wearing very little.

''See, maybe if I did something more with my hair,'' Lilah said, lifting her hands over her head to shove her taffy-colored tresses high. Several long strands slipped out and kissed the soft pale curve of her neck. ''I might look more exotic.''

With her arms over her head, her breasts lifted enticingly. Tyler felt a surge of heat plunge through his body. He was instantly hard and hot. Damn it, this wouldn't do.

Dropping to his knees beside her, he reached out and caught her hands, gently bringing them down to her sides as her hair cascaded around her.

''You don't want to be exotic, Lilah.''

She raised troubled blue eyes to his. ''Well no, I don't want to change myself for good. I just want people to actually believe that some man who isn't simply looking for a quiet little wife might be interested in me.''

''They'll believe,'' he promised on a whisper. ''And you don't need to change a thing about yourself. You're lovely just as you are.''

She quickly retrieved her hands and folded them in her lap. ''I wasn't looking for compliments.''

''Someone should have been giving you more of them. You don't sound as if it's something you're used to.''

''I suppose I'm not. I've always tended to hide behind a reserved facade. I like being quiet most of the time, but the first impression men usually get is that I'm standoffish or dull. I'm not the type they want to play with.''

''Mmm. Just the type they want to marry.''

''That's not always a compliment when it means someone thinks you're manageable or settled or boring. When a man wants one kind of woman to play with and another to bear his children, well, I don't think that man meets my requirements.''

She stared solemnly up at him. Tyler realized that he had become one of those unsettled men who chose women he wanted to play with. But then, he would never choose a woman to bear his children. Life had taught him it wouldn't be fair to the woman—or the children—to promise a forever he couldn't provide.

''You're a beautiful woman, Lilah,'' he said. ''If some of your beauty is on the inside and men don't see that, it's their fault and their loss.''

''Maybe. And maybe I'd like to have some idea how to bring the inner me to the surface.''

''We will.''

She stared up at him silently for several seconds. Finally she sighed. ''You really think this crazy plan will work?''

He lifted one corner of his lips. ''Are you trying to tell me that you *can't* help me find the information I need?''

Sudden sparks of indignation rose in those mesmerizing blue eyes. Her cheeks turned pink with the implication of his words. ''I most certainly can help you. I dare you to find anyone who can do the research better than I can.''

Tyler couldn't help but grin. ''Lilah,'' he drawled, ''I do believe your insides are showing. You're looking decidedly excited. One might even say 'hot' or 'exotic.'''

A low chuckle slipped from her lips. ''I know what I'm good at, and, yes, I have more than my fair share of pride when it comes to my known accomplishments. I suspect you realized that and tried to get a rise out of me on purpose.''

''Maybe I did. It worked, anyway, didn't it? You looked like a woman with fire in your soul.''

"Hmm, but you can't keep me angry all the time."

"I don't intend to, but I'll tell you this much. You know your way around a research project, and I know how to create a buzz around a man and a woman. When we're through, the men in town are going to know that you're a woman with a very interesting soul."

"You really believe you can turn me from Goldilocks to The Lady in Red?"

"I'd bet my reputation on it, sweetheart."

"And what will you pay if you lose the bet?"

"You choose."

She opened those fine eyes wide, concentrating hard. Finally she cocked her head. "If we succeed as well as you believe we will, I'll plan a week of treating you to the best that Sloane's Cove has to offer as your reward. If you can't deliver what you've guaranteed, you'll agree to a week's worth of community service in the cove."

"Community service?"

She nodded. "Sure. As a member of the local business association, I know that we're always looking for ways to improve the community, and it takes a lot of hands to make a town work."

"All right, then," he said, rising to his feet and reaching out to pull her up beside him. "Let's start right now."

"Right now?"

He stroked one long finger down her cheek. "Backing out already?"

She raised her chin. "I'm more than ready, Tyler."

"That's good," he said, pulling her to the door. "That's very good. Hold on, now. Look at me as if you love me."

He pushed the door open, stepped out onto her doorstep and pulled her close beside him. He tipped her face up to his and angled his mouth over hers.

Her knees gave way almost immediately from the shock and from the very feel of him pressed close against her, the heady touch of his tongue when it slipped between her lips.

Tyler caught her and held her, her body tucked against the long, strong length of him.

Finally he let her go. He winked.

''Be ready for me at seven o'clock,'' he said. ''I intend to make this a night to remember.''

And he smiled and left her standing there. When her head finally cleared and her vision finally recovered, Lilah looked up to see several people gathered on her walkway.

Alma was chief among them. The woman was grinning wickedly.

''Way to go, hon,'' she said. ''You're looking a little flushed and woozy right now, and you don't have that much time to get ready, so I won't ask for details this moment, but don't think I'm not going to descend on your store in the morning. I want to know everything that happens tonight.''

Judging from the crowd around Alma, she wasn't the only one who was interested in what was going to happen tonight.

As Lilah moved back into her house, closed the door and leaned back against it, sliding to the floor, she had to admit that she wanted to know what was going to happen tonight, too.

Her telephone began ringing almost immediately after Tyler left, but Lilah refused to pick up the phone.

It wasn't like her to act that way, not at all, but if she talked to the wrong person, her resolve might weaken. With great boldness, she switched on the answering machine, determined to be strong and keep her hands away from the receiver.

For the first time in years she felt as if something wondrous and exciting was about to happen to her. Not that she didn't love her life. She did, but it was decidedly stimulating to get to play at being someone else for a while.

The answering machine kicked on. "Lilah, what in hell do you think you're doing?" Her brother Frank practically yelled. "This isn't funny anymore. You're playing with double-action dynamite. Anything could happen. Bad stuff. You don't know what guys like Westlake are like. You haven't had any experience with his type."

"And that's the absolute truth, dear brother," Lilah whispered, as Frank gave up in frustration and banged down the receiver. "I'm about to do something new and daring."

She squeezed her eyes shut as she shimmied into a butter-yellow sheath and picked up her brush to try to do something with her hair.

By the time she had finished getting ready, every single one of her brothers had left a message, ranging from Bill's touching, "Oh, hon, don't do this," to Hank's "For God's sake, at least take along a can of pepper spray and a cell phone so you can call one of us if you need us." She thought she heard Hank's wife admonishing him to "Leave the poor girl alone and let her have some fun," but then the line went dead and she was left sitting there wondering if maybe her brothers weren't a little right.

''Could be getting in over my head,'' she muttered.

But then the memory rose up of John Claxton explaining that she was lucky to have him asking for her.

''Oh, well, glug-glug,'' she said. ''If I'm going to drown, at least my body will be found naked and in Tyler Westlake's possession. Nothing boring about that.''

If she hadn't been alone, she would have laughed out loud at the thought. As it was, she tried not to do too much talking to herself, living alone as she did. It was bad enough that people thought her boring. No cause to let them think her insane, as well. So she sat quietly waiting for Tyler, wondering what she would do if he changed his mind. Alma and a small crowd had heard him say he was coming for her tonight. If he didn't show, Lilah didn't even want to think of the humiliation. It was one thing to never have a man look at her with desire. It was another to have a man pretend to desire her madly and then decide she wasn't worth the trouble.

By the time it was five to seven, her nerves felt as if they were stretched like the rubber band on a slingshot.

When the doorbell rang, she felt her breath stall in her throat. She jumped to her feet, then thought better of looking too desperate to her neighbors. Carefully she smoothed her damp palms down her sides, then made herself go slowly as she walked to the door.

It creaked just a bit when she opened it, as if to signal her neighbors, ''Here he is. At last.''

But when she opened the door, all thoughts of her neighbors fled. Tyler was smiling down at her, his green eyes sparkling.

He reached out and ran long, strong fingers down

her bare arms, the slide of his skin against her own nearly making her gasp. Suddenly the conservative yellow dress seemed dangerously revealing.

''You're lovely,'' he said.

She tried to regulate her breathing. ''I'm scared.''

Slowly he shook his head. ''Don't be. It's just you and me, and I knew you when. Remember? Remember when I used to come to this town and this island, just a tall, gawky kid with too much arm and leg?''

She didn't remember him that way. ''The local girls must have liked all that arm and leg. I seem to remember Linda Barnsworth sighing as she wrote your name all over every scrap of paper she could find. She practiced kissing you in the mirror.''

He chuckled. ''I'm honored. I *do* hope I was a gentleman and behaved accordingly when I was around your friend.''

''You said hello to her once and she refused to let any of us talk to her for three days. She said that she wanted to remember your voice and only your voice. Five years ago she married and moved to Pennsylvania, but she tells me that when her husband misbehaves, she lies and tells him that Tyler Westlake wanted her real bad when she was fourteen.''

Tyler gazed down into the soap-scrubbed face of Lilah Austin. He could have told her that the only young woman he'd had a crush on ''real bad'' in those last years when he was visiting the island was her. Unfortunately, she'd been too young for him at the time, a full three years his junior. Not to mention the fact that his mother had discovered his secret and had decided that he'd be better off spending his summers learning the business than mooning over ''one of those Austin girls.'' She'd been right, of course. He would only have caused Lilah Austin grief if he'd ever revealed his secret crush. As things stood now, he was an adult and well aware of the consequences of his actions. A man who couldn't offer a stable relationship had no business trying to start something with a woman who was looking for the right man to build a life with.

"All set to shake up the men of Sloane's Cove?" he asked, holding out his hand.

She placed her hand in his, and his fingers closed around her. "Make me dangerous, Tyler," she whispered with a small smile.

But he could have told her that she was already plenty dangerous. If other men didn't see that, there was something very wrong with their eyes and their testosterone levels, because he felt a definite unnerving jolt just at the feel of her hand in his.

As he led her down the stairs and past his car, she looked up, a question in her eyes.

"We want people to see us together. Walking will provide more opportunities than driving. Besides, if we walk, I can add to the illusion we're trying to create by doing this," and he slipped his hand around her waist. She gasped slightly, and he knew she wasn't used to men claiming her this way. He wasn't used to his own reaction, either. The warm curve where her hip flared out was incredibly distracting, but he smiled down at her encouragingly. He'd promised to make her look invitingly dangerous. To do that he had to touch her, no matter the cost to himself.

"You do that very well," she said quietly. "Must be lots of practice."

More than he wanted to think about right now. "I thought perhaps we'd eat at an outdoor café, if that's all right."

"So that people can see us?"

"Yes," he said tersely, thinking that he'd like to take her somewhere where no one could see them at all.

"Eating?"

Her voice was so incredulous and slightly affronted that he couldn't help shoving his own discomfort aside. He looked down and saw that there was a small frown between her eyes.

"You don't like to eat?"

"Of course I like to eat, but it doesn't seem very... dangerous, does it?"

He laughed out loud, the sound echoing down the street. "Lilah," he drawled, "just talking to you on a telephone could be dangerous. Watch, I'll show you."

He gently led her down the street to the outdoor café at the Sloane's Cove Inn, where he requested a table practically on the sidewalk.

"Look at me," he whispered when she was seated across from him. "No, don't look anywhere else. Not at the people passing by on the sidewalk, not at the waiter, not at the menu."

She stared directly into his face steadily, her blue eyes trusting and so soft that he wanted to kiss her eyelids closed and do what he'd said he wouldn't do. Make love to her right here and now.

When the waiter arrived, Tyler didn't look at the man, either. He ordered wine and scallops.

"How do you know I eat scallops?" she asked when the man had gone.

He smiled, still not looking away. "I don't, but this is Maine. I don't have to look at the menu to know that scallops will be available, and if you don't like them, I can always offer that as an excuse to spirit you away later under the guise of feeding you again.''

He reached out and looped his hand around hers, stroking her fingers with his thumb.

''Lilah,'' he said in a slow drawl as he lowered his lips to kiss the fingers he'd been stroking and then the pulse at her wrist that was fluttering wildly. Immediately he moved away from that dangerous territory. She was not unaffected by his touch, and he was certainly pushing the edge of his own limits by touching her this way.

When their wine arrived, he picked up her glass and held it to her lips so that she could sip.

''Okay, brace yourself,'' he said softly, almost beneath his breath, and he didn't know if he was talking to her or to himself.

He leaned forward across the small table and kissed the wine from her soft lips that automatically molded to his as if that mouth had been waiting for his kiss for all time. Instantly heat, arousal, the desire to crush her to his chest and fit her body to his own, slammed through him.

A small murmur escaped her lips as they parted. He could press on, he could take what she was allowing him. And he could risk losing control completely.

He wavered, he fought the urge to close his palms around her shoulders and drag her close. It was a battle he almost didn't win, but finally he released her.

With a dark, heated look, he rose and tossed several bills down on the table, more than enough to cover the cost of the dinner and a very generous tip for the waiter.

''Let's get out of here, angel,'' he said, his voice rough and thick.

She didn't protest as he led her away and back toward her house. Once they were safely inside again, he took a deep breath, then looked at her with some concern. There were twin frown lines between her delicate brows.

"You okay?" he asked.

Lilah nodded slowly, as if she were uncertain. Her eyes were slightly troubled. He wanted to run his fingers over those frown lines and soothe her, but he didn't dare touch her again, after he had almost let things get out of hand back at the restaurant.

"Are you sure you're all right, Lilah?" He couldn't keep the concern from his voice.

This time she took a deep breath and nodded a bit more forcefully. "What do you think people are thinking?"

He thought people were probably thinking that he was plunging his body into hers right now, but no way was he going to say that.

Instead he raised one brow. "What do *you* think?"

She shook her head. "You don't really think people will believe you were so eager to take me home that you didn't even stay to eat the food you'd ordered?"

Tyler raised one shoulder. "We're here, and I haven't eaten."

His words brought a trembling chuckle to her lips. "You're right. We haven't eaten, and now we're trapped in here for a while. What should we do?"

Anything but touch, he thought.

"Eat," he suggested. "Plan our next move."

"Take the phone off the hook," she agreed. "I can pretty much guarantee that my brothers will be calling if we don't. And as for the planning, I'm not sure there needs to be a next move, do you? That is, maybe we've already achieved our goal? I only wanted to shake people up a bit.''

She was no doubt right. If they'd jolted all the young studs into seeing her as a woman and not just a well-mannered breeding machine, there'd be no reason for the two of them to continue on.

''Of course, I haven't done my part yet,'' she added. ''Maybe we should get started on that right now. I'll bring some food and we can start going over what we already know about your mother's house. Then tomorrow—well, tomorrow we'll see what happens.''

''I agree,'' he said carefully. ''Tomorrow we'll venture into town and see what kind of reaction we've gotten. Let the gossip begin.''

Chapter Five

"Lilah, that man has got the kind of eyes that just make a woman want to lie down right in the middle of town and lift her dress. How in the world did you ever manage to keep breathing when he was kissing your fingertips last night? I still had the fruit stand open and I saw everything. I practically pulverized the tomatoes I was putting in a bag for Mrs. Ennis. She had to find two more to replace them."

Alma had slipped into Lilah's bookstore and had immediately pulled her into the storage room, whispering her comments and trying to peek out the half-opened door at the same time.

"Alma, what are you doing?" Lilah asked. "I can't stay in here talking about Tyler. I've got customers."

Her friend practically snorted. "Customers, hah. Only two or three of the people out there are actually looking for a book. The rest of them are just waiting for Tyler to show up and take a good taste of you again. The two of you have certainly jazzed things up in

Sloane's Cove. Only the tourists are oblivious to what's going on, and even some of them are probably wise to the vibes zinging around the bookstore today.''

Lilah smiled and shook her head. ''Alma, your imagination is running wild. I'm not arguing that people wouldn't be a bit interested in what Tyler does with his time when he's in town, but I honestly don't believe they're going to hang around my bookstore just waiting for him to show up and kiss me.''

''You're right. Some of them are here—the men, I mean—because they want to see if they've been missing something. Look at that. It's so pitiful. Joe Rollins is trying to read that book upside down. I guarantee you, he's just looking for a new set of lips to kiss, and he's decided that yours might deserve a second look.''

Lilah felt a small surge of alarm at that. Joe Rollins was, and had always been, notorious for kissing and telling and then kissing someone else and telling again. He had never, and would never, have looked twice at a woman who didn't have the reputation of being a bit fast.

''Maybe he's just looking for something good to read,'' Lilah argued.

Alma gave her that ''honey, please don't embarrass yourself this way'' look. ''The man has been known to openly brag that he never reads anything that doesn't have pictures of naked women.''

Sure enough, Lilah noted that the book Joe was looking at was a biography on Rubens. She didn't even want to begin to wonder why he was looking at nude paintings upside down.

She also noted that there were quite a few more men in the store this morning than there usually were.

Cautiously she started to step back into the store, but Alma caught at her arm.

"So?"

Lilah turned and looked at the anxious look in Alma's eyes. "What?" she asked.

"So, how was it, sweetie?" Alma asked. "I mean, I'd assumed it was beautiful, but you're not exactly looking as if you're going to sprout wings and fly out of the bookstore this morning. You're okay, aren't you, hon? The man didn't hurt you, did he? He *does* have a bit of a reputation with women."

For the first time since last night, Lilah allowed herself to assess her feelings—just a bit. Last night she'd been caught up in Tyler's magic. The man truly did have gifted fingers and lips and a voice that could coax a woman to do…oh, just anything. When he'd kissed her fingers, she'd thought she would just slide right out of her chair, and when he'd touched her wine-dewed lips with his own and slid his hand behind her neck, her mouth had felt so hot. And then she'd been back at home. She'd remembered that this was all a show, a sham, a means to an end. There'd been a sad sense of disappointment at first. Which was completely silly and unrealistic. She knew what she wanted, and it wasn't someone like Tyler. She just wanted an ordinary man, all her own, who wanted her back. She wanted to be valued, to be really noticed for once. That was Tyler's plan, to make sure men saw her as someone to be noticed.

Judging from the crowd just outside her door, his plan had worked really well.

"I'm very grateful to Tyler," she said without thinking.

Alma raised her brows. "He was that good, was he?"

Lilah couldn't keep from laughing. "We didn't do what you think, Alma, but we *did* talk for hours. He's a fascinating man, you know, and I'm not talking about the way he kisses."

Her friend practically snorted.

"Well, yes, he certainly can kiss," Lilah said, trying not to imagine that hot, hungry mouth on her own, "but I'm talking about who he is. He's got all these brothers and sisters that he adores, and they all work together on the restaurants, all of them doing their own part. Tyler's part is the research and renovation. His St. Louis restaurant was once an old schoolhouse, and he's salvaged the stove and the bell and as much of the rest as he could. He studied the history of the school and has anecdotal information and photos posted around the restaurant. The hostess acts as the schoolteacher. The tables look like desks. He loves his work. You can tell when he speaks about it. His eyes…his eyes…"

Lilah realized that Alma had gone very quiet and that *she* had been doing all the talking—about Tyler.

"Well, he's dedicated," she said abruptly. "And he's bringing in workers to start the renovation on his mother's house soon, so we had plenty to talk about all last night."

"You talked all night?"

Alma's voice was a little too incredulous, a bit too loud. A few people in the store turned around to watch.

They *had* talked all night. Lilah felt her face growing warm. While she was just fine when she was with Tyler, playing his game, she wasn't actually very good at lying about their arrangement.

"What do you think?" she asked her friend, and she knew her face was flaming red.

Her friend studied her carefully. Then Alma smiled. "I think any woman who spends half the night with Tyler Westlake and tries to convince anyone that all they did was talk has probably got a big mountain to climb. Who would ever believe that?" Alma asked.

There was something in her eyes that told Lilah that Alma *did,* in fact, believe just that. They'd been friends long enough to read each other's expressions at times. But it was obvious that Alma knew she had her reasons for wanting to pretend she was hot stuff with Tyler, and as a friend she was more than willing to play along.

"Go see to your customers, hon. Your young man is here, anyway."

Indeed, Tyler had just entered the shop. His head was up. He was gazing around as if he was searching for something.

Lilah left the room and headed his way. She had only taken two steps, however, before she was stopped by John Claxton.

"He's toying with you, Lilah," John said. "A man might want to sample the bread, but is he going to actually buy the loaf? Think about that before you do something foolish again."

"Think about how you're speaking to the lady, Claxton." Tyler's voice echoed softly at her back. "Lilah's a sweet, generous woman and a good friend to most of the people here. She's an asset to the community. People might not think too kindly of someone who insults her."

A general low murmuring of agreement ensued, and John Claxton flushed red.

"I didn't mean it as an insult to Lilah," he insisted.

Lilah took a deep breath. John Claxton was studying her intently. Darryl Hoyne, a terribly shy but very nice man, was pretending to read a magazine while gazing at her over the top as if he'd just discovered she kept a halo beneath her pillow, and Joe Rollins was grinning knowingly. He put his book down and sauntered over her way.

''Maybe John doesn't appreciate your finer points, Lilah, but most men would notice them right away.''

She felt Tyler stiffen at her back, and all of a sudden Lilah felt like laughing. Joe Rollins had never looked at her other than as someone to copy work from when they were in school.

''Thank you very much, Joe, but I'm sure John was only looking out for my welfare. Good morning, Darryl,'' she said. ''Let me know if I can be of any assistance.''

In the space of just a few seconds she slipped back into the role she knew so well, that of devoted businesswoman.

''Mrs. Ransom, are you finding everything all right?'' she asked an elderly woman who was thumbing through the bestsellers.

''Oh, yes, most fun I've had in the bookstore in years. Don't you let those men start a fight in your store. They can just take it outside if they want to duke it out over you. The thought of them messing up all these lovely books, well, it just wouldn't be right.''

And suddenly everyone was shuffling about and looking guilty.

''I'll call you, babe,'' Joe Rollins said as he moved out the door. Darryl followed him, nodding his head in greeting as he went. John Claxton had already shuffled out of the store while Mrs. Ransom had been speaking.

When the room had calmed down, Tyler took a step closer. ‘‘Everything all right?’’ he asked, studying her calm expression.

‘‘I'm fine,’’ she said, nodding her head, and it was the truth. Their experiment yesterday hadn't exactly had the desired effect. She now had one angry suitor who still wanted a mother for his children, one man who she suspected wanted her to do something that would involve getting naked and throwing away her dignity. But in Darryl she also had garnered the interested glances of a man who might prove promising. She should have been somewhat excited. As it was, she didn't feel much different than she normally did…except for the fact that her arm was tingling where Tyler was standing close beside her.

He leaned over and placed his lips near her ear.

‘‘Mmm, you smell nice,’’ he said, loud enough that a woman standing nearby dropped her book. ‘‘And we need to talk,’’ he said in a much quieter whisper.

She glanced up at him and saw that his eyes were worried.

‘‘I'm really fine,’’ she told him, ‘‘but yes, I do believe we have something to talk about. The store closes at five and I have a few things to do at home, but if you could, I'd like you to meet me here at six. I have something very interesting I want to show you.’’

As her words faded away, Lilah realized that the buzz in the store had dropped to nothing. Twenty pairs of eyes were turned toward Tyler and herself. She realized she'd just invited him to meet her in a dark, empty store so that she could show him something.

He smiled, showing even white teeth, then brushed one finger over the tip of her nose. He leaned close again.

"You did that very well, even if you didn't mean to."

Then he turned toward the door. "I'll see you at six, Lilah. Wear something short. It's going to be a warm evening."

"This is fantastic stuff," Tyler said, looking at the photos Lilah held out. "Where did you find all of these?"

Lilah shrugged. "Collecting old bits of local history is a hobby of mine. A few years ago, when we had our annual summer festival, I went around bugging all the locals to hunt out some of the photos they had buried in the attic. I'd forgotten I even had these two. I'm pretty sure it's what your mother's house looked like one hundred years ago. No columns, see? Those were added later. I haven't figured out when, but I have some ideas on places I can look to find out. I also have some leads on someone who might be able to dredge up some information about former inhabitants of the house. Maybe even a diary."

"You figured all that out in the space of a couple of days? Lilah, you're incredible. These photos alone are phenomenal, but I don't want you to knock yourself out doing this. You've got a business that takes up your days, and—"

"And this is the third time this week you've given me your nights," she said softly. "Fair is fair. Besides, I get the fun job."

Tyler ducked his head. "You're not implying that I'm not having fun doing my part?"

She kept her head down, pretending to be studying the details of one of the photos. "Not work, exactly, but well, let's be honest, you could be out actually dating someone instead of *pretending* to be dating someone.''

''Oh, yeah, it's incredibly hard work kissing you.''

Those lovely blue eyes flashed silver sparks. ''I'm not completely naive, Tyler. I know this isn't like pounding on a rock pile or anything, but I—''

''Lilah?''

''Yes?''

''Hush.'' He pulled her close and kissed her. ''You're not completely naive, but I have to let you know here and now that I'm not even slightly immune to your allure, just in case you thought I was doing a really fine job of faking it. Maybe you're right that you have the easier task of the two of us, because, in case you haven't noticed, you're an incredibly attractive woman, and I'm—well, hell, I'm incredibly attracted. The fact that we wouldn't suit is neither here nor there. It just means I can't follow things through to their natural conclusion. It means that you have to keep your eye on me to make sure I don't try to push things further along than you feel comfortable with, but never, ever make the mistake of thinking what I'm doing here with you is even remotely related to work.''

''You do it very well, though, I have to tell you. Just in case you thought I was completely immune, as well. I'm not.''

Tyler groaned at the softness in her voice.

''And while we're being completely honest, you should know that I once had an incredible crush on you,'' Lilah said.

He smiled and brushed her hair off her face. ''Me, too.''

''You never said.'' Her eyes widened with surprise, possibly even disbelief.

"I was seventeen. You were fourteen. You were too young, and then—" He shrugged. "I got sent away. My parents always had very rigid ideas about life. Employees were to know their place, and so were Westlake heirs. My mother made it clear that she'd married for position, that she'd borne me for duty, and that I was to devote myself to the Westlake name and business. If I was wasting my days mingling with the citizens of Sloane's Cove, I obviously had too much time. It was decided that I should begin learning how to run the family empire."

Immediately a sad look came into Lilah's eyes. "You were unhappy then?"

He smiled and stroked a gentle finger down her cheek. "It was a long time ago. I'm past it."

She still looked slightly troubled. "You're happy?"

He smiled. "No one has called the shots for me for a while. The choices I make are strictly my own. I live a life that suits me."

"I know. We're very different, aren't we? You're meant to run an empire and dazzle a dozen ladies a month. I'm meant to stay in one place with one man for an entire lifetime."

He nodded. "We're different. Entire lifetimes don't work for Westlakes. We don't have the knack for constancy, at least outside of business. Not a nice thing to admit, but true."

"You do nice things. You make people happy with your restaurants, and I'm sure you make many women happy in a single year. That's not so bad."

He smiled. "I'm not the one we're concerned with right now, and we still don't have you where we want you yet. That wasn't exactly progress we saw this morning. Who was that Joe guy, anyway?"

Lilah laughed. ''Joe Rollins? Someone who wants me naked.''

His hands froze on her arms, and green ice formed in his eyes. Lilah watched as Tyler visibly forced himself to relax. He let go of her and took a step back.

''Every man wants you naked, Lilah, but I take it Joe's not the one?''

''No,'' she said, shaking her head, ''but it was nice to be allowed in the line after all these years. I've never been just a sex object.''

He gave her that deadly look again. ''And what about that other man?''

''Darryl,'' she said, studying the matter. ''Darryl I'll have to think about. He's smart, he's steady, he's just a bit shy.''

''Don't make the mistake of thinking his mind isn't ranging along the same road Joe Rollins travels.''

''You sound like my brothers now,'' she said with a small laugh.

''I'm beginning to sympathize with your brothers. Still, I think I made a tactical mistake last night. We want men to see that you have a dangerous, adventurous side, but a romantic side, as well.''

Lilah's stomach started to roll at the implications of what Tyler was saying.

''I thought maybe we'd done enough,'' she said quickly.

''You're not taken yet,'' he said softly.

''No.''

''Then we're not done yet.''

She couldn't stop staring at his lips. She was dreadfully afraid she was going to lean forward and ask him to kiss her, and there was clearly no reason for him to kiss her, since no one else was around.

Finally she dragged in a deep breath and nodded.

A pounding at the door had them both turning toward the sound. Lilah started to move toward the store's entrance.

Tyler touched her arm and halted her progress. "It's after hours. Are you expecting someone?" When she shook her head, he stepped in front of her, taking three long strides across the store to unlock the door and pull it open.

He looked down at a near duplicate of Lilah—except for a slight difference in eye shade, a subtle difference in demeanor.

The lady raised one brow. "Hello, Mr. Westlake. I didn't expect to find you here. Lilah wasn't at home, so I assumed she'd be at the store."

People seemed to make a lot of assumptions about Lilah, that she would marry a man she hadn't chosen, or in this case, that she had nothing to do with her life outside of work and home. Interesting.

He raised one brow right back, and the lady laughed. "Okay, like I should talk. With the baby and Jackson and writing recipe books all day, I don't get out much myself. Less than Lilah. It's just—you know, the twin thing. I knew she was probably here."

"Good to see you, Helena," he said with a grin as he moved aside to let her in. "Your sister's right here," and he pulled the luscious bundle that was Lilah from behind him. She wasn't exactly smiling.

"I could have gotten the door," she said.

"I just wanted to make sure it wasn't Joe Rollins."

Helena whooped. "He's got that man's number, Lilah. The whole town is talking about what happened at the bookstore this morning, complete with Joe leering at the chubby naked ladies."

"They were Rubenses," Lilah explained.

"I know. But it doesn't matter, because we all know that Joe wasn't looking at them because he'd taken a sudden interest in Flemish painting. He was probably imagining you in those portraits, minus a few pounds of course."

"The man is a swine," Tyler said.

Lilah frowned. "He's a harmless swine, though. And it's not like you to go all overprotective on me, Helena. You know I'm not going to let Joe get that close."

"Of course I do, but it's not Joe you have to worry about. It's someone else. Four someone elses."

A groan slid from between Lilah's teeth. "They're not planning anything drastic, are they?" She glanced up at Tyler with a worried look in her soft blue eyes.

"Like removing significant body parts from Tyler? Probably not *that* drastic. No, more like they're simply putting their heads together for the next barrage of men. They're pretty sure Tyler isn't a real candidate."

Tyler couldn't help himself. He gazed down at Lilah and stroked one long finger down her cheek. "Looks like I'm not doing what I promised I'd do. I'm losing the bet, too."

"Bet?"

Tyler smiled at Helena. "I have a real interest in making sure Lilah is treated fairly. What kind of community service did you say I might be doing if I fail?" he asked, teasing a smile to Lilah's eyes.

She shrugged. "Oh, could be anything. Planting flowers in the flower boxes. Carrying packages for little old ladies in the shopping district. Sweeping the sidewalks? Servicing lonely shopkeepers?"

That last unexpected line startled a laugh out of him. "And what do I get if I succeed?"

She thought a minute. ''A moonlight sailboat ride. A homemade meal by the best cook in the area,'' she said, nodding toward her sister. ''Lunch at Jordan Pond. Sunrise on Cadillac Mountain. Whale watching.''

''Guess I'd better think of a better plan, then.''

But he knew that his desire to help Lilah had little to do with their business deal and even less to do with their bet. He simply didn't want to see her bullied. He'd seen too many people pushed around by life and other people. His parents had been good at that sort of thing, just as good as they'd been at moving from one relationship to another. He'd inherited some of their flaws—but not all.

No one was going to push Lilah around.

But as he walked to his car later that night, he gave himself a shake.

''Don't kid yourself, Westlake,'' he said to himself. ''This isn't just some altruistic idea you have here. You want to help Lilah, but it doesn't hurt a bit that helping her means you get to touch her.''

And sometime soon his lips and Lilah's would get acquainted again. He was already hungry for that moment.

Chapter Six

Three days later Darryl was in the bookstore again and so was Avery Munson, who was Lilah's banker. Lilah looked up from the customer she was helping and found Avery studying her intently. The banker had always been helpful and friendly, but nothing more. He had never looked at her as if she'd grown bigger breasts. He was looking at her that way now. Not in a leering kind of way, but it did appear that he hadn't actually noticed her as a woman before, and now he did.

He saw her staring and smiled pleasantly. She smiled back, but her heartbeat didn't speed up.

Maybe later, she thought. Avery was a good man. So was Darryl.

Darryl finally chose a history of the American West and brought it to the register.

"I hope you enjoy this," Lilah said. "It's just come out."

Darryl's ears turned a bit pink. ''I always was interested in the western migration.''

She hadn't known that. She supposed she hadn't known much about Darryl and hadn't really bothered to find out. Lilah felt a stab of guilt.

''Let me know how you like it,'' she said, but Darryl had obviously used up his conversational reserves. He grabbed his book and fled.

Five minutes later Avery paid for the latest issue of *Financial Notations* magazine. ''It's almost time for us to schedule our quarterly business meeting,'' he told her. ''I'm really looking forward to it. Maybe we could discuss things over lunch this time.''

His smile was slightly nervous. Lilah knew she could hurt his feelings. ''Lunch it is, then, Avery,'' she said, and instantly wondered if she'd said the wrong thing. He was a nice man, but she didn't feel anything but ''nice'' when they spoke.

Maybe in time. No doubt she would feel more if she and Avery got to know each other as people instead of business associates.

''Something to think about, Lilah,'' she finally ordered herself moments later, but her mind just couldn't wrap itself around the idea of herself and Avery ever ending up undressed and in the same bed at the same time. Never mind the fact that she'd dreamed of Tyler tall and naked and carrying her off to bed just last night.

She slammed the cash register drawer too hard, then glanced apologetically at the customer she'd been waiting on. ''Sorry,'' she said softly as a few people turned toward the sound.

''Looks like you've got men coming out of your

cash register,'' one customer said. ''Which one of those guys is it gonna be, Lilah?''

Lilah smiled at the elderly man who had chuckled as he asked the question.

''You know you're the only man I'd have, Elliott,'' she said.

''Poor souls,'' he said with a wink. ''But I don't believe a word of it. That Tyler Westlake has half a chance, I think. At least he knows that he's supposed to kiss the girl instead of offering to look at her bank book.''

His comment drew a laugh from the customers, but it made Lilah squirm inside. She realized people *had* assumed Tyler's ruse was real. They might also assume that he was deserting her when he finally concluded his business and left the cove. There might be bad feelings. His new restaurant might even suffer.

The thought made her suck in a deep breath.

Natalie, one of her summer clerks, looked at her strangely.

Lilah suddenly turned to the young woman. ''Would you mind watching the store alone for an hour, Natalie? I have to see someone.''

Natalie raised her brows. ''No problem, Lilah.''

Lilah tried to pretend she wasn't blushing and that she left the store midday all the time.

But the knowing look in Natalie's eyes told her that the clerk and everyone else suspected just where she was going. There would be questions afterward.

Tyler looked up from the roof tile samples he and the contractor were going over and saw a vision in blue and white walking toward him.

''Excuse me,'' he said to the man. ''I think we're

agreed on what's needed. If you have any questions, you know where I am.''

The man laughed. ''In a bit of a rush, are we, Westlake? Well, I can't blame you. You look like a man who's seen a mirage, and maybe you have if that's Lilah. She never leaves her store during business hours. Must be something pretty important to bring her out this way.''

That was what he was afraid of. As she drew near, he saw that Lilah's eyes were wider than usual. Did she look a bit flushed?

He moved toward her, meeting her far enough away from the house that their conversation couldn't be overheard.

''Are you all right?'' he asked, catching both of her hands in his own.

She smiled then. ''Yes, I'm perfect.''

He twisted his lips up in a smile. ''Well, I'm glad we're agreed on that, anyway.''

Lilah frowned. ''You know that's not what I meant.''

''Hmm, what exactly did you mean then? Something happened?''

''Avery Munson asked me to lunch.''

His fingers froze on her own. ''Avery Munson?''

''He's a man I know.''

''Really? What kind of man?''

''A man my brothers didn't send my way.''

''And he wants…lunch? You're happy about this, then.'' He didn't even want to know why he was having to struggle so hard to keep from squeezing her delicate fingers.

A pale-pink blush colored her cheeks. ''Well, I do feel a bit guilty about not being more excited about

Avery's invitation. It's just that he's my banker and I've never thought of him in any other way before. Anyway, he wants to discuss business, but we've never had lunch together in the five years we've been working together. It means something.''

Tyler wanted to say that it meant the man was an idiot if he'd waited five years to ask her to lunch, but that would have been mean...and not the whole story.

''It probably means he's finally gotten the courage up to do something he's been wanting to do for a long time, angel,'' he said, realizing that it was no doubt the truth.

She crossed her arms. ''I don't know about that, but I do know that it means you don't have to keep dating me. We can end this right now, and no one will think anything of it. Especially if I go out on a date with Avery.''

He raised his brows, but before he could speak, she went on. ''Don't think I'm trying to back out on my part of the bargain, though.''

He didn't. His first thought, in fact, had been a simple ''Not yet,'' but no doubt that was simply primal male instinct making itself known. The truth was that maybe it would be best if he eased out of Lilah's life. He'd been enjoying this masquerade too much for his own peace of mind.

''In fact, there's news about your house,'' she rushed on, her eyes glowing. ''This morning one of the calls I've been making paid off. I've found someone who's a collector of historical memorabilia. A good friend. He's got information on some of your ancestors.''

Tyler keyed in on the one bit of information that had hit home. ''A good friend?''

Lilah wrinkled her nose. ''No, not good in that way. He's not a potential mate.''

He wished she hadn't used that word. It brought up visions he was better off not envisioning.

She was gazing up at him with that little-girl smile that took his breath away, practically dancing while standing still. ''When can we go?'' she asked.

''We?'' he teased. ''I thought you'd done your part. You found the info. That makes us even.''

''Ty-ler,'' she drawled. ''Please.'' And that one word coming from her lips made him want to touch that mouth with his own.

He took a deep breath, fighting for composure. ''I take it you want to come along?'' he asked, knowing he probably should say no. If they were going to end their bargain, it would be best to clip things off quickly. If she was going to begin a relationship with another man, that man probably wouldn't care to share her with someone she'd been kissing lately.

She tapped him lightly in the chest with her fingertips. ''Do I want to come along? Are you kidding? Of course I want to come along. Don't you just love this kind of treasure hunt?''

''Oh, yeah,'' he agreed, gazing down into those beautiful, excited blue eyes. He did love the hunt. He always had, but at the moment it wasn't the hunt for buried history that was foremost on his mind. He simply loved looking at her when she was this way. ''Just let me sign out of here,'' he said, automatically taking her hand and leading her over to where a man wearing a T-shirt and jeans sporting a number of holes was scraping paint off the outside of the house.

''Danny, I've got to leave for a while,'' Tyler said,

and the man turned around on his ladder. He spotted Lilah and gave a low whistle.

''Hey, no problem, Ty. You just go off and play now. I'll stay here and take care of all the work,'' he said with a grin.

The look on Lilah's face was precious. Her eyes were wide, her lips were parted in surprise.

Tyler chuckled. ''Lilah, meet Danny O'Hara. Lilah Austin,'' he added, by way of introduction. ''Don't pay any attention to Danny's bossy ways. It's part of his natural charm. Besides, he knows I have to be nice to him. Can't do this job without him. He's my right hand,'' Tyler explained.

''And a grateful right hand,'' the young man said, bowing slightly while he clung to the ladder with one hand. ''I hope you'll forgive me if I tease. It's good teasing. Tyler found me raiding garbage cans when I was sixteen and a dropout and no one would hire me. He picked me up, offered me a high-paying job on condition that I let him send me back to school, and I've been with him ever since. I would never betray this man. Usually. This one has pretty blue eyes, though, Tyler. For her, I might betray you. If only I weren't already married.''

Tyler grinned. ''That's loyalty for you. To me and to Rosellen.''

''She knows I adore her.''

''You're lucky she adores you, too. You'll be okay here?''

The man nodded. ''All we're doing is prep work today. Not many decisions to make. Go on. Enjoy Ms. Austin's lovely blue eyes. Nice meeting you, Ms. Austin,'' he said.

"Call me Lilah," she said. "You're obviously a friend of Tyler's, and Tyler's been a friend to me, too."

He smiled. "Then we have something in common, Lilah," he said. "Don't you be afraid to tease him, either. He needs teasing now and then. With his money and his reputation, people think of him as larger than life. They don't always treat him like a real person."

Tyler laughed. "Danny's been taking classes at night. Last semester's course was interpersonal relationships. All of us who know him have served as guinea pigs. We better get you out of here before he begins to analyze every word you say."

"Hey, you don't want to admit the truth of my words, but—" Danny shrugged. "Be real for him, Lilah," he urged.

She stared up at the man for a second and then she gave a quick nod. She called a soft goodbye as Tyler led her away. The walk to the car was quiet.

"Don't look so somber," Tyler said. "And don't put any stock in Danny's words. He may look like a young stud, but he's a mother hen at heart."

As he tucked her into the car and joined her, he realized she hadn't answered his comment.

"What are you thinking?" he asked.

She looked up straight into his eyes. "That in spite of the fact that you came to the cove for several summers, I never really knew you. Just the image. Just the fantasies that every young girl likes to make up about handsome young men she doesn't know anything about."

He laughed then. "Don't worry. There wasn't much to know. I spent my winters in Baltimore, my summers here for a while. I moved between two parents, went to school, learned the family business, went to work, followed the family tradition of marrying and divorcing, and decided to concentrate exclusively on what I do best, which is this,'' he said, gesturing toward the stately building in the process of being reclaimed.

''Doesn't sound like much fun.''

He laughed. ''Lilah, haven't you heard? I'm the king of fun. When I'm not working, I play. It's a tradition in the Westlake family, and I excel at it.''

Still, Lilah thought, watching his face as he pulled out onto the road, Danny's words haunted her. She knew Tyler's reputation perfectly well. She knew he liked to tease and laugh, and she'd heard plenty about his women and his family's predilection for hasty marriages and divorces, but she also knew that Tyler championed those unable to champion themselves. He liked history, he loved his work. There was a depth to him that he tried to keep hidden. She wondered why.

Unbidden, a memory of a lean, teenage Tyler came to mind. Tall and handsome and smiling, he'd attracted the attention of the local females just as he still did. And remembering a day when he'd picked her up off the ground when she'd fallen off her bike, she realized he'd had that gallant streak even then.

The ''wall'' had existed then, too. The sense that he was of one world and she was of another, worlds that could only intersect for a short time. No long-term connections allowed.

''Something's bothering you,'' he said gently, and she shook her head, although he was right. She didn't want him being forced to be gallant for her right now. Not when it was her turn to give to him. A lighter tone was in order.

''I'm just trying to pretend I ride in one of these all

the time,'' she said, smiling as she motioned to the Maserati.

''You should. Seated in this decadent car with the wind whipping your hair about, you look a bit wild, Lilah.''

''I am wild,'' she said in a teasing, low voice. ''And dangerous. Haven't you heard?''

''I've heard. And so has everyone else. The men are starting to get wise. I'll have to run them over with my car if they get out of line.''

''I thought we wanted them to get *in* line.''

''Exactly. They've got to behave if they're going to take you out.''

''Have you been talking to Frank?''

''Only in my subconscious. You're sure this Avery's okay?''

''Avery is very safe.''

Tyler raised one brow. ''Maybe not. Maybe now that he sees you as a desirable woman, he'll forget himself.''

There was a slight frown between Tyler's brows.

Lilah laughed. ''Thank you, Tyler.''

''For what?''

''For believing that a man would lose his head around me. You're the only one other than my brothers who thinks I could be responsible for a man undergoing a serious personality change.''

''Don't assume the man's personality has changed. He's probably always noticed something about you, but now he's aware of the competition. It's called forth the animal inside him.''

''No personality change?''

''A dog that gives up barking is still a dog.'' Which sounded a lot like a warning to her.

"You're right. Avery is still the same gentle man." She said the words with affection, and Tyler nearly slammed on the brakes. He slowed to a stop in the middle of the deserted road.

"He's a man, Lilah, and he's a man who's been awakened to you as a woman. A desirable woman. Be careful, angel."

His voice was low and raspy, and she studied the dark-green of his eyes.

"You're feeling guilty," she said with surprise.

"When we began this, it seemed like a good idea. I didn't like what your brothers were trying to force you into, but I don't want men thinking you're easy prey, either."

Lilah couldn't help smiling then. She placed gentle fingers on his own, wrapped tightly around the steering wheel.

"I'm a big girl, Tyler. I know all the synonyms for the word *no,* and I've read enough self-defense books to have a clue what to do if I got into a bad situation, but you don't have to worry, anyway. Avery might have urges, but he's not the kind of man to force himself on a woman."

She stared directly into his eyes. Seconds passed.

Finally Tyler shook his head slowly. "I don't like it, but all right, you've made yourself clear, Lilah. I wanted you to get fair treatment. That means I can't play the let's-tell-Lilah-how-to-live game any more than your brothers can. For the record, I *am* glad you're getting what you want," he said, then he eased the accelerator down.

"Let's conclude our business deal," Lilah said. "Looks like I'm going to have to pay up on my bet."

* * *

Greg Bisby's house was a huge blue hodgepodge of different styles that had been added on over time, making the building look like a period-piece sampler. The graying man met Lilah and Tyler at the bottom of his porch.

"Come in," he said solemnly. "I've got the stuff inside."

Tyler noticed that Lilah moved readily into the house and didn't even look around once they were inside. As if she'd been here many times before. The shades were pulled, the pale-lemon light barely filtering in.

"It's to protect all the documents and photos, Mr. Westlake," the man said, though Tyler hadn't asked. "They're delicate and one of a kind. Not as valuable as children, but they need to be treated with care."

"You're a man who cherishes his history then," Tyler said, knowing this was a man to respect despite his odd, dark house.

"I collect it. I study it. That's why it was no problem at all locating something about Sea Watch when Lilah called me."

He held out a faded blue diary, slightly torn. In his other hand he held a small stack of newspaper clippings as well as a few photos and something that looked like a ledger.

"Births and deaths. Records from a church that was torn down years ago. You'll want a place to sit," he said, and directed Tyler and Lilah to some overstuffed maroon chairs close by the one window where the shade had been raised.

Tyler smiled. "I wouldn't mind putting this diary and the church records under glass to display in the restaurant."

Lilah chuckled. ‘‘Go ahead and try. You’ll see just how a gentle man can turn into a stubborn bull. I’ve tried to get Greg to part with some of his treasures before. Never works.’’

‘‘Maybe if you’re good and don’t get in too much trouble, I’ll leave some to you in my will,’’ the man said, but he was looking at Tyler. It was clear by that ‘‘getting in trouble’’ comment which road Greg Bisby was taking. He’d heard the stories about Tyler kissing her silly in town. He didn’t want anyone taking advantage of her any more than Tyler did.

‘‘I think you’re a very wise man, Mr. Bisby,’’ he said. ‘‘Thank you for letting me look.’’

‘‘I’m happy to comply, as long as looking is all that you do. Some things are easily damaged.’’

‘‘Some things are to be treated with the greatest of care,’’ Tyler agreed.

‘‘Some men are to be seen and not heard, especially when they start interfering in other people’s lives,’’ Lilah said, looking up like a queen into Tyler and Greg’s faces.

Tyler chuckled. Greg slapped him on the back. ‘‘She’s a cool one,’’ Greg said. ‘‘I shouldn’t have worried. Now I’ll just leave so you can read all about the Westlakes and what eventually became of Sea Watch.’’

One hour later Tyler and Lilah traded documents, and an hour after that they looked up at each other, dazed from reading in the dim light and from a surfeit of knowledge about Tyler’s family.

‘‘Well, I see my ancestors were no better than the present bunch of Westlakes,’’ he said with a wry smile. ‘‘My great grandmother left her husband and returned to South Carolina to marry again. My great grandfather had three wives and numerous mistresses.’’

"And a prosperous business building boats. No wonder you're such a natural at renovating old buildings. That background in woodworking."

Tyler shrugged. He'd been aware of how the family business had evolved. He'd even been aware of the numerous marriages and mistresses, but reading about it firsthand in a diary made his family's circumstances more real.

He hadn't come here to dwell on that part of his past. "What do you know about old boats?"

"A little," she said, but her eyes took on that romantic glow.

"I've never renovated a boat. Might be fun."

"We're in Maine. Surely you can find a worthy project. It would be...romantic, don't you think? Your family's business coming full circle. It would make a great story while people enjoyed their meal."

He smiled. "I'll have to think about that. After Sea Watch."

"Sea Watch is going to be beautiful. I can tell already, just from what we've unearthed today. You'll immortalize the story about your grandfather personally escorting the clock all the way from Switzerland, won't you? Do you think we can find any trace of the clock? Greg told me that most of the original furniture is gone."

"I have the clock. In New York," he said slowly just to savor the view of her eyes lighting up.

"I'd love to see it. Of course, I will if you put it in your restaurant." He remembered again what she'd looked like as a young girl, how he'd considered asking her inside the gates one day, but then he'd remembered. His mother was inside. She would make someone from the Cove feel uncomfortable. She knew how to freeze people out. She did it frequently to make a point, and she always made her point. It mostly worked. He rarely got too close to anyone from Sloane's Cove when he was young. It was only once he had grown that he became rebellious and risked hurting others.

Lilah's eyes were still dreamy, he noted. No one had planted shadows there. He would hate for anyone to do that.

''What was it like living at Sea Watch in the summers?'' Lilah asked suddenly. She was staring down at an old photo. His great-grandmother had apparently commissioned a photographer to immortalize the rooms in the house.

''It was a beautiful place, but very quiet,'' he said slowly. ''My brothers and sisters are all products of my father's other marriages. I was the only one who came here with my mother. She worshipped the house and the wealth it stood for. Every year on the first day back, she'd lead me through the house, reminding me of my duty to my position.''

''Did you—'' Lilah's soft voice faltered. She shook her head.

''Ask,'' he said.

''It isn't really any of my business. It's not my right to demand you satisfy my curiosity.''

''It's my right to decide what I'm willing to tell you.''

''Did you marry for duty?''

At last he smiled grimly. ''The exact opposite. I defied my family by marrying Julie, who was warm and innocent and with absolutely no background. Within a year I'd become like every other Westlake. Too much business, too little everything else. I brought her in to defy history, but I ended up repeating it. Fortunately for me she married again. She's happy.''

''People make mistakes, Tyler. Did you love her?''

''I liked her immensely,'' he said. It hadn't been enough. He wasn't at all sure that what Avery Munson was offering was good enough, either. A woman ought to be treated as if she were the most special woman in the world. Especially if that woman was a man's wife-to-be.

''I want to see if I can find out more about your grandmother's quilt collection,'' she said. ''She talks about donating some of them to various institutions. I wonder if any of them still exist.''

''I wonder if we can't encourage Avery to do the right thing.''

Immediately she was wary. ''He asked me to lunch.''

''To talk business, you said.''

She lifted those long lashes, enabling him to see the consternation in her pretty blue eyes. ''Oh, well, that's Avery. He's very into business.''

Tyler knew about men who placed business too high on their list. Hadn't he just warned her about such men? If the man couldn't be induced to provide her with a little romance, he didn't deserve to have her.

''Maybe he just needs a little education.''

''Oh, I don't think—''

''I do. And I have an idea of how we could show Avery how a woman like you should be treated. Tomorrow night you and I—''

She put one hand out. ''I told you, you've done enough for me, Tyler. We're even.''

Slowly he shook his head. ''I did nothing. You did all this,'' he said, motioning to the treasures she and

Greg had unearthed. ''This would normally take me months of searching.''

She gave him one of those ''I don't believe you'' looks, which made him laugh.

''And the quilts. Don't forget the project you're planning,'' he pointed out.

''Are you trying to protect me again, Tyler?''

''Maybe a little,'' he said, his voice growing low and husky. ''Indulge me, Lilah. I'll feel better if you do.''

''You shouldn't worry about Avery. He's just a friend, just a nice man.''

''That's what you told me you were looking for.''

''It is.''

''Then it's what I want for you, too. And don't tell me I've already won the bet. You haven't achieved your goal yet. I could still end up potting roses.''

He stood, taking her hands and pulling her to her feet.

At his mock-sorrowful tone, she gave in a bit, shaking her head and smiling as she leaned back, gazing up at him. ''Or emptying the garbage cans after the summer festival. We always need a few hands for that job. Could be terrible.''

''You're right. Something terrible could happen if you don't go out with me tomorrow night.''

''Something terrible?''

He nodded.

''I'd hate to be responsible for making you lose the bet. We'll go out then. For your sake. And Avery's,'' she added, glancing back at him over her shoulder as she moved away and called out their thanks and good-byes to Greg.

They were nearly to the car when Lilah turned around again. ''Tyler?''

He cocked his head, waiting.

''What are we trying to show Avery, exactly?''

Tyler leaned forward from the waist. He brought his lips close and kissed her just beneath the delicate line of her jaw, tipping her head up. He slid his hand behind her waist.

''We're trying to show him how to treat a woman he desires. A man does not ask the woman of his dreams to go over her bankbook at lunch.''

Lilah dragged in a deep breath. She gave him a slow, shaky nod.

''What exactly does a man do with the woman of his dreams?''

He grinned then. ''I'll show you. And Avery. Tomorrow night. Lesson number two. If the man wants you, he had damn well better be prepared to deserve you.''

Chapter Seven

When Tyler handed her onto the yacht he'd reserved for the evening, a luxury number with room for ten guests and ten crew members, Lilah felt her hands begin to shake. There were no other guests, just her and Tyler. She was reminded for the first time in a long time of just who he was and who she was.

She was the daydreaming young girl who ran into walls when he came around. He was the confident son of James and Lucille Westlake, child of privilege, heir to the Westlake dynasty, a man who attracted women the way rock stars attracted groupies. Several of those women were lounging near the pier right now, sending her furious looks. Maybe they knew that this wasn't real and they wanted her to get out of the way so that they could step in and be next in line.

Maybe she should do just that.

But she glanced up that moment into Tyler's green eyes. He was looking as if this were the most exciting moment of his life. She'd never, ever had anyone look at her as if she were personally responsible for making their evening special.

Probably hundreds of women have seen that look, she told herself. But she smiled, anyway. Why shouldn't she enjoy this evening with Tyler? It would never come again.

"All set?" he asked.

She nodded. "What is all this?" she asked, motioning to the yacht.

"Setting. Magic. A mood maker."

No question about that. The gentle rolling of the deck beneath her feet, the breeze off the water, the gathering dusk, the gorgeous man gazing down at her possessively, all were making her head spin just a little.

"You're lovely tonight," he told her. His low, deep voice felt like fingers skimming along her skin, dipping beneath the narrow straps of her short, pale-blue dress.

Lilah took a deep breath. "You're lovely, too."

"Do me a favor. Don't tell Danny that. The temptation to analyze your words would be just too tempting, but thank you."

The slow heat of a blush climbed her skin, but Lilah didn't apologize. In stark black and white, his broad shoulders nearly blocking out the sky behind him, Tyler *wasn't* exactly lovely. But he *was* incredibly handsome. He was the kind of man that made a woman want to push her hands beneath the lapels of his jacket and slide her fingers up his chest.

"I've never been on a vessel like this," she said suddenly. "Not this large, anyway. Not one that was privately owned. Where are we going?"

He slowly shook his head and took her hand, leading her to a table located near the bow. The table was covered in white linen with silver candlesticks and silver-edged china. The flames of slender white candles reflected in the crystal. A bottle of wine rested in a basket. ''We're not going far tonight. Close enough that anyone standing on the shore can see and make a report to anyone who might be interested, far enough away that we can't be heard if we keep our voices low.''

''Scene setting,'' she said, dropping her voice to match his.

''Exactly.''

As if he'd given an order at that moment, when he'd done nothing of the sort, the captain called out to let them know they'd be leaving port. Tyler made sure she was safe and seated at the table. A short distance out they made anchor.

Immediately a crew of waiters appeared. Wine was poured. Crusty French bread and green salads were served.

Tyler held out his glass to hers.

''Here's to your happiness, Lilah. To getting all the good things you want and that you so richly deserve.''

She touched her glass to his. She sipped at her wine and stared into his dark eyes. The sky grew less bright around them.

''What do you want out of life, Tyler?''

He smiled slowly. ''You and Danny have something in common. He asks me that question all the time.''

''And what do you tell him?''

Shrugging a shoulder, he took another sip of his wine, leaned back in his chair and gazed directly into her face. ''What I tell him doesn't usually please him.''

''I'm not asking you to please *me*.''

''What are you asking?''

''Talk to me. That's all. We're out here for hours. Talk to me.''

''All right. We'll talk. I don't have great aspirations if that's what you mean. I like my work. I want to do it well. I want to ensure that my brothers and sisters are gainfully employed and cared for. I want to have time now and then to gaze at the stars.''

She looked up at that, although only a few stars were even faintly visible yet.

''They change a bit from location to location,'' he said. ''But they still remain constant. Always there when a man looks up.''

''Stability's nice,'' she agreed. ''I know a lot about it.'' And she smiled to show him that she wouldn't step over the barrier that he obviously didn't want her to cross. The things he'd mentioned were all important, but they weren't very personal. They didn't delve into the heart of the man. She was pretty sure Tyler didn't want her looking into his soul. It was a painful thought, but she respected his choice.

''What else do you know a lot about?'' he asked.

She stared down at the shining white of the tablecloth. ''Books. History. Maine. Family.''

''You want children?''

''Of course,'' she replied, as if that shouldn't even have been a question, but she looked into his measuring gaze and realized that it *was* a question to him. She supposed it was a question he'd already answered by deciding he wasn't going to have children. He'd given up on marriage. He enjoyed his life alone. It suited him.

''Think carefully about whom you choose, Lilah. Not every man will make a good husband or father. Even if he cares for you, a man might not be suited to the task.''

"Choosing a husband isn't something I take lightly, Tyler. If that were so, you and I wouldn't be here doing this."

He smiled then. "What are we doing, exactly?"

She smiled back. "Eating?"

Both of them laughed, because though their salads had been waiting for them for several minutes, neither of them had taken a bite.

"We'd better eat something," she said. "Your poor chef will be chewing his fingernails thinking we don't appreciate what he's prepared."

"Paul will understand. He's dined with a woman or two in his time. Quite the lady's man."

"Did you pick him up off the street, too?"

He shrugged noncommittally, and she knew that he had, but that he wouldn't betray his friend by carrying stories.

"We'd better eat," he agreed, "although this hasn't been without its plus sides. By now everyone on shore will want to know what fascinating topics we've discussed that have kept us from our meal."

They ate, they talked, they laughed. He filled her glass again, and then after only half a sip, he stood, pulling her from her seat and straight into his arms.

Soft music began to play. Something low and hot and jazzy. He swirled her close, and her body molded tightly against his.

"I don't dance very well," she whispered.

"You don't have to. My mother insisted I learn to accommodate any woman no matter what her abilities might be. Westlakes do not embarrass themselves on the dance floor," he said sternly, and she knew it was the voice of Lucille Westlake he was imitating. She'd heard the woman lecturing him once in town on the proper way to open a car door for a lady. His jaw had been set tightly, his chin raised in embarrassed defiance.

But he'd learned his lesson awfully well, she thought, remembering the way he always took care to make sure she was safely tucked inside his car before he closed the door. He knew how to exert just the right amount of pressure so that the lock clicked shut but there was no jarring crash of metal against metal.

''What are the keys to making sure every woman feels comfortable in your arms?'' she asked, trying not to blush and failing miserably.

He chuckled and brought his lips close to her ear. She'd parted her hair on the side. Tyler slid his fingers into her hair and pushed the tendrils aside. ''In a perfect world, I hold you tightly enough and close enough that you don't stumble,'' he whispered, moving his hand on her waist just a touch so she could see what he meant, ''but far enough away so there's no question of anything improper.'' Again, he splayed his fingers wider against her waist, demonstrating the immovable distance between them.

''Still—'' he said, leaving his sentence unfinished. She pulled back slightly to look into his eyes.

''Still?''

''This isn't a dancing lesson tonight. It's a lesson of another kind. For an avid audience,'' he said, nodding toward the not-so-distant shore and the few people lounging there. ''I should hold you closer.'' And he drew her in slowly, until her breasts were nearly touching his chest, her hips barely separated from his. She could feel his warmth from shoulder to knee.

Lilah took a deep breath. She reminded herself that this was just for show, but still she closed her eyes.

She tried not to think about what it would be like to dance with this man every night, to be the woman he had chosen. Foolish to think that way when he'd already made it clear that he would never choose one woman. She was only the woman for tonight, and even then, only because he was trying to help her the way he'd helped Danny or Paul. If she opened her eyes she'd have to face that reality, and so she didn't. While Tyler waltzed her around the perimeters of the deck, she simply reveled in the joy of flying in his arms, of being held close to his heart.

When the music stopped, he released her. Slowly.

"Thank you," he said, and his deep voice was slightly unsteady.

She wondered what he'd been thinking while they were dancing. Maybe he was thinking about the woman he used to dance with, the one he'd married and, in his opinion, failed.

But he'd come here tonight to do a good deed. He deserved a bit of levity. Lilah blinked wide. She laughed.

Tyler studied her. "What?"

"You're thanking me? I'm a woman with two left feet, and for a moment there I was sailing. I was fluttering my wings. I'll bet I could interview a thousand women who've danced with you and they'd all be grateful for your expertise." She curtsied before him as best she was able in a skirt that was much too short for such things.

"Thank you, Mr. Westlake, for your expertise in the ballroom. I'm experiencing all kinds of new things tonight. My first time on a yacht, my first time to eat dinner on deck, my first time to dance without counting my steps or worrying about permanently maiming my partner.''

''You couldn't do that,'' he said with a shake of his head and a smile of disbelief.

''Humph,'' she said with a slight wrinkle of her nose. ''I've broken the bones of bigger men than you, Tyler Westlake,'' she declared.

She'd said that last a little more loudly than she'd intended, and her eyes widened as she realized that probably everyone on shore could still hear her. He gently placed his hand over her lips and pulled her close.

''Uh-oh, now everyone will think that I've done something wrong and you're threatening me with bodily harm. How are we going to dispel that notion?''

''I wouldn't want anyone to think that you'd scared me or that I felt threatened by you in any way,'' she said softly, and closing her mind to how bold and unlike herself such an action was, she looped one arm around his neck and drew his head down to hers.

Their lips met. Once. Twice.

He angled his head and took her mouth more possessively. She surged into him, held onto him. One foot left the ground and her slip of a high-heeled sandal slid off.

Tyler lifted her into his arms so that she wouldn't lose her balance. Slowly he ended the kiss and carried her to a bench.

In the short time they'd been dancing and talking and kissing, more stars had come out of hiding.

''We need more time,'' he whispered hoarsely. She knew that he meant they needed more time to make a convincing romantic picture to their audience, but she just wanted more time to be with him this way.

"Show me the stars," she whispered back.

He nodded wordlessly. He pulled off his jacket, draped it around her shoulders and eased his arm around her.

"That's Hercules," he said, pointing to a series of stars. "He's a warrior, a hunter. And there's plenty for him to hunt in this night sky. Leo, the lion," he said. "Hydra, the nine-headed serpent, Draco, the dragon." He showed her each one as he named them.

"Is he a successful hunter, do you think?" she asked softly.

"He's successful. He gets what he goes after."

Like Tyler, she thought. If he wanted almost any woman, he could have her. But he had to want her first. And in this case the woman had to accept the fact that she could only have him for a few weeks or a few days or even a few hours.

She wondered if this evening had been a success. It had certainly been romantic. But she wasn't supposed to be having romantic thoughts about Tyler, was she?

"Wow, I was perspiring watching the two of you last night," Alma said, leaning over the counter where Lilah was down on her hands and knees looking for the bags she'd somehow managed to lose. She'd managed to lose a lot of things the last few days, she reminded herself. Her mind, her common sense, every self-protective urge she possessed. Had she really kissed Tyler Westlake last night without him even asking her to?

If she ever found the bags, maybe she should put her head in one. What had she been thinking? But she knew the answer to that. She hadn't been thinking at all. She'd just been feeling.

"Ouch," she said, finally locating the bags and rising too quickly. Her head hit the side of the counter slightly.

"Alma, you weren't really standing on the pier watching us, were you?"

"Of course I was! You get on a yacht with only a small crew of men and one of the biggest playboys on the East Coast and you expect me not to worry? Or to watch? I wasn't the only one, either. Pretty much everyone in this store passed by at one time or another last night. Not much happening on TV, you know. Summer reruns."

Lilah couldn't help smiling. "Well, I'm glad everyone in Sloane's Cove found entertainment for the night then. Happy to oblige."

"Well I wouldn't say that everyone was entertained. Your brothers were ready to call out the coast guard. And there were more than a few women who were looking as if they'd eaten nails for dinner. Come to think of it, there might be one or two of them in here this morning. Better watch your back...and your books."

"I will. Thanks, Alma."

Her friend was still studying her. "What?" Lilah asked.

"Was it fun?"

She smiled to herself. "It was—" For a moment the bookstore and all its inhabitants disappeared and she was remembering the feel of waltzing across the deck, held against Tyler's heart, the way his lips had burned a trail of fire down her throat when he'd kissed her good-night before he'd taken her ashore. But she looked up and saw a huge circle of interested, eager faces, and suddenly she didn't want to share, even though sharing the experience had been the intent of the whole thing.

Her night with Tyler felt too personal, too close.

"It was a very satisfactory evening," she said primly, and Alma nearly snorted.

"Taking your dog for a walk at night is a satisfactory evening," she offered. "Watching your favorite TV show is a satisfactory evening. Tongue wrestling with Tyler Westlake has got to be better than that, or the man's just not doing it right."

Instantly Lilah felt deep indignation and a sense of protectiveness rush over her. "Tyler is definitely doing it right," she said, her voice bouncing off the books and the shelves and the walls.

A long-haired, long-legged redhead flashed Lilah a furious frown and stormed out of the bookstore. A pretty blonde gave Lilah a knowing look and then headed for the exit. Lilah wondered just how well the women knew Tyler. It didn't take much to figure out that they would be waiting in line for their turns.

"I'd watch your back today, sweetie," Alma said. "Wish I could stay, but I've got to get back to the fruit store before my clerk eats all the blueberries."

When Alma had gone, Lilah suddenly felt naked. People were still staring at her. Total strangers and people she'd known her whole life. She'd spent a lifetime working up enough poise to be able to follow her dream of opening up her own bookstore, but now all her calm had fled. She hadn't a clue what to say to get from this deeply uncomfortable moment back to the old, easygoing, laid-back atmosphere of a normal day at the store.

Take deep breaths, she ordered herself. Remain

calm. Think about the books. Just the books. This is your store, your home, your haven.

Slowly her mind settled down, her thoughts stopped running for the door. This *was* her kingdom, and she loved it. She knew these people, her customers, and what they wanted and needed.

A satisfied smile formed on her lips. She started toward a new customer who looked as if she needed some assistance.

The sound of someone clearing his throat noisily stopped her.

''Lilah?'' The throat clearing hadn't been all that effective. Darryl's voice came out as a cross between a whisper and the creaking of a door. He was blushing furiously when she turned to him.

Lilah aimed a sympathetic smile his way. She knew too well the pain of embarrassment. ''Do you need some help, Darryl?''

He nodded slowly, then shook his head furiously. ''Yes. No. Not exactly. Could I talk to you a minute?''

''Of course.'' She looked up, waiting. ''Is there…a book you needed?''

He leaned forward slightly. ''Could I talk to you alone?'' He lowered his voice to an ineffective whisper.

She froze.

Someone dropped a bag.

Darryl was looking as if he'd just said the completely wrong thing and knew it.

He'd done nothing wrong. Sympathy rushed in. Lilah nodded slowly. ''Of course you can. Let's step into the office.'' She led him through the door where few besides herself ever went. For half a second she remembered that this was where Tyler had kissed her the first time.

She stumbled slightly, and Darryl had to jump aside to keep from banging into her.

"Sorry," she said.

He finally smiled. "That's okay. It's all right to be clumsy. I am. At times."

She turned to him then, prepared to ask him what he needed, to make things easier for him, but it was as if Darryl had run out of time.

"Would you go to the movies with me this Friday, Lilah? I'll understand if you don't want to," he said all in a rush.

Lilah blinked. She looked up at this painfully quiet, painfully shy man she'd known all her life and wondered how much courage it had taken him to ask that simple question. He was a good man. He was the kind of man she'd said she was looking for. The kind of man she really should get to know better. But...

But nothing. Tyler wasn't real. He was a good man just as Darryl was, but Tyler wasn't even remotely available. He was like one of those stars. Mesmerizing but unreachable. A terribly temporary man, maybe even a slightly bored man, who was making his time here a bit more interesting with a bit of well-placed benevolence. Nothing wrong with that, except she wanted...

She shook her head to chase that half-formed thought away.

"I'm sorry. So you don't want to go to the movies. Okay." Darryl started to turn away.

Wasn't he the very kind of man she'd told Tyler she was looking for? What kind of woman was she to be dithering now that the opportunity was here? Tyler had given her this gift. It was his skill and his arrangements that had made Darryl even notice her.

"Yes, I'll go to the movies with you," she said, just as Darryl was opening the door.

He turned and looked at her as if she'd gone crazy. Then he nodded. "Good, then. I'll pick you up at seven Friday night."

He went out the door. She heard the ringing of the bell as he left the store, and then a buzzing as if a lot of bees had just entered the bookstore.

Lilah opened the door wide. She stepped outside, and everyone stopped talking again.

Nervousness rose in her, but this time she refused to give in to it. She took a deep breath.

"All right, yes. Darryl is taking me to the movies. Now can we get back to normal here?"

Her announcement jarred the people in the store and brought a chuckle and a round of applause.

"That's a lovely idea, Lilah," Mrs. Seaver said. "Especially since we're fifteen minutes overdue for the reading circle. I think it's very nice that you have so many young studs panting over you, but please, let's not forget the books. Let's definitely get back to normal."

Lilah wished it were that simple. She didn't feel normal at all. She wondered what Tyler would say when he heard the news. Would he be happy? Would he admit that they had accomplished their goal this time? If so, he'd have no real reason to see much of her after this.

A strange deep pain ripped through her.

Too much excitement, she told herself. She wasn't the type for all this excitement.

"Let's begin," she said, forcing herself into the circle of chairs she'd set up. She waited for all the other members of the reading circle to join her, then she picked up her book and began to read.

She would lose herself in the magic of print and she would not, definitely not, think any more thoughts of Tyler.

No matter what else happened this morning. In spite of her silly comment that she wanted to be dangerous, the fact was that too many wild and crazy things had happened lately, throwing her off balance.

Surely today she'd had her quota of dangerous and risky. What else could happen?

Chapter Eight

Tyler opened the door of Lilah's bookstore and wondered what had happened. No people milling about. No men proposing. No soft sounds of pages flipping.

What he did hear was the low, sweet sound of Lilah's voice and the silence of twenty women seated around her in a circle of chairs, their gazes focused completely on her face.

She was looking up at him, the small tinkling sound of the bell on her door just fading away. For three seconds her eyes met his. Then she smiled and nodded just a bit.

"Lilah, what happens next?" a woman's voice asked.

"Yes, you can't stop there," an elderly woman added. She looked at Tyler. "Mr. Westlake, come have a seat. Lilah's got the reading circle now. Come listen."

Instantly Lilah raised her eyes. "Oh, I don't think—Tyler, I won't be long. Really. Just—"

He smiled slowly. ''I'd like to hear. I've never taken part in a reading circle before.''

Those blue eyes narrowed slightly with concern, but she didn't say no. Finally she nodded tightly. She looked down at the book resting on her palms.

He waded into the circle of women. Two of them flipped their skirts aside so that he could sit on a narrow chair between them.

''She's very good at this,'' one of them whispered.

''Shh,'' the other one said, as Lilah's voice and the story she was reading captured Tyler's attention.

> ''The wind whipped Dahlia's dress around her ankles, and she loved every touch of the silk against her legs. This was her first long dress, her very first dance, the first time she would ever be permitted to allow a man to hold her in his arms while the music mesmerized, and she planned to enjoy every single second.''

For half a second Lilah faltered. She glanced up into his eyes as he focused intently on her, but she quickly recovered and returned her attention to her book.

The story was of forbidden love, first love, and Lilah's voice swelled with passion as she read. When the heroine's heart broke, Lilah's tone grew thick with unshed tears. When the hero knew he'd almost lost the woman of his heart and despaired of ever getting her back, tension grew in the urgent, soft whispering sounds that fell from Lilah's lips.

Tyler leaned forward in his seat, caught up in the moment, amazed at how much he wanted to walk across the circle and kneel at his quiet little bookseller's feet. She lingered over every word and lived every emotion. He was sure of it. Listening to her make love to the story was like savoring warm chocolate, feeling it slowly melt away against the tongue. That tantalizing sensation of wishing the moment would last longer, the way a man felt when he made love to a woman, driving himself to completion and bliss, yet wanting to hold on to the sensation for as long as possible. He listened and watched her every move. He drank in the sight of her pale-blue-and-white dress, her long slender fingers fanned out to hold the book, her rich voice drawing in her audience, stroking nerves and imaginations and ending on a long whisper as the chapter concluded.

The woman next to him sighed. The lady on the other side turned to see his reaction. He could see her from the corner of his eye, but he couldn't turn. Not yet. Lilah hadn't raised her head. It was as if she had thrown every ounce of her soul into the reading, as if she had been drained of her very essence.

''Lilah,'' he said softly, the syllables echoing in a long, drawling caress. ''Look up, angel.''

The woman on his right patted his hand. ''Don't worry, dear. She'll be back among the living in a second or two. Lilah's a true vessel of the written word. We could all read this book ourselves, of course, but it just wouldn't be quite the same. Our Lilah's a master, but it takes a lot out of her. She feels what those characters feel. For the short time she's reading, she lives the book.''

He could see that, but that didn't make him stop worrying.

Tyler started to rise, but just then Lilah took a deep breath that lifted the bodice of her white lacy dress trimmed in icy blue. She quickly raised her head and smiled directly into his eyes.

"I'm back," she said with a small chuckle. "Sorry. I really do try to make this a performance."

He slowly shook his head. "You could take the stage and make your fortune."

Her eyes widened with something like horror. "Oh no, that's not me. Just here. Just this small group of my friends and neighbors. And the words," she said, glancing down at the book and smoothing her hand lovingly across the linen cover. "It's really the story that makes the difference."

He could have argued, but he knew she'd argue right back. For all her sweet, quiet ways, there was a little streak of stubbornness in Lilah. It was that hint of gentle daring that had allowed her to kiss him last night. The memory of that moment when her petal-soft lips had risen to meet his still made his body stir. And he was definitely already stirred up enough this morning after listening to Lilah's voice. He wondered how many men had been caught between the reality of her prim little businesslike persona and her love-me-until-I-see-stars voice.

Tyler stifled a groan of frustration. He managed a small laugh. "We'll just have to agree to differ on that one. It's not just the book."

He rose then and moved toward her as she got to her feet. "Having a good morning, sweetheart?" he asked, and he could swear he heard someone gasp slightly. It wasn't him, and it wasn't Lilah.

"Wait till he hears," he thought he heard someone else whisper, but the sound was very low, very hushed.

He wanted to ask what all the whispering was about,

but clearly it was a secret from him. He couldn't ask out loud. Not here.

"Can you leave for lunch?" he asked, holding out his hand. "Would that be all right?"

Again, the gasp.

Lilah stared at his hand as if she were afraid to touch it. Then she shook her head as if she was pushing aside those same fears. She raised her chin.

"I'm the owner, free to do as I please with whom I please," she reminded him, but at the sound of muffled mumblings that followed, he had a feeling there was a deeper message that was being conveyed here.

Deliberately Lilah placed her hand in his. "Natalie?" she asked.

"Covered. No problem. Go for it," Natalie said with a quick thumbs-up and a smile.

Together, quietly, he and Lilah left the store. They walked down the street, her soft hand in his as he forced himself not to move a finger and risk that sizzling sensation that did him in every time his skin rubbed against hers.

"Quiet morning?" he asked nonchalantly.

She chuckled. "Um, I guess you noticed that there was a bit of tension in the store today."

"Your brothers?"

"Actually, no, although I'm pretty sure they'll show up sooner or later. But no, first there was a lot of whispering about what you and I were doing last night. Lots of wondering where your hands were roving when we were watching the stars. No one thought I could hear the whispering, of course."

"Of course." He leaned close. "Good morning, Lilah," he said, kissing her earlobe.

She dragged in a deep breath, then looked up at him guiltily.

"I guess I should have already told you that you don't have to do that anymore."

A stab of something that felt a whole lot like staggering disappointment zipped through him. "No?" he asked carefully.

"I have a date Friday night."

No, that wasn't disappointment. Disappointment was mild and slightly sad. This was the kind of thing that made a man clutch his chest and fight for breath.

"With Avery, I take it?" he managed to say. He hoped he sounded encouraging. There was no point in sounding any other way. Avery had things to offer that not every man could offer. Something any Westlake male who'd ever lived could never offer. Things like stability and forever.

He nodded his agreement, but she was shaking her head.

"Not Avery. He hasn't been in yet. Darryl asked me to go to the movies."

"I see." The movies. Sounded simple. Sounded tame. The kind of thing that everyone did. Teenagers went to the movies. Where it was dark and a man could sit close and would have to bring his lips close to whisper if he wanted to talk. A place where a man could touch a woman easily if the mood was right.

"Well then, that's good," he said, hoping his smile looked sincere. "He's a good man, you said, didn't you?"

"He's a very good man," she said firmly. "And—I think—a deeper man than I realized."

The howling started deep inside Tyler's body. A long, slow no-o-o-o funneled through him. He had learned early on, though, about quelling his emotions, about never showing his deepest feelings. He was a master at shoving his wishes into the background, when he had to be. Now was one of those moments when he had to call on the lessons of his youth.

Not just to protect himself this time. To protect her, which was ten times more important.

"I'm happy for you, Lilah," he said, and he realized that he was. The fact that he was unhappy for himself didn't matter. He had nothing to offer, nothing he really wanted to give. This was good. And right. "You see, angel, they were all just waiting for you to spread your wings and give them the signal that it was okay to come close."

She stopped and smiled up into his eyes. A small, sweet and slightly confused sort of smile.

"I've never had this kind of relationship with a man not related to me," she said slowly. She reached out and took his hands. She studied them. "I wish I'd known you for real when we were children."

It would have been a mistake. If he'd known her, he would have wanted her, and his mother had been right when she'd told him that his family shouldn't mingle with the locals. His family, his situation would have chewed Lilah's sweetness up and killed it. But still, he wished the same thing that she did.

"I'm going to love seeing you find what you're looking for," he said softly. "Shall we have lunch? Maybe by the ocean?"

She smiled. "I'd like that. You can tell me what's going on with your house today."

He nodded tightly. "You can tell me about this man who's going to take you to the movies on Friday."

Lilah rolled her eyes. ‘‘Are you pulling an ‘Austin brothers’ on me?’’

‘‘Lilah,’’ he drawled. ‘‘I’m just protecting my own interests. If I lose our bet, I’ll be taking out the trash on Main Street.’’

He wasn’t exactly lying. He was protecting his own interests in the sense that it would make him happy if she were happy. He wanted her to have the best man available.

Darryl Hoyne had darn well better treat her right or there was going to be hell to pay.

Lilah couldn’t wait to get to Tyler’s house today. She’d spent the past two days poring through every scrap of history she had that pertained to Sloane’s Cove. Last night, she had come across something interesting. The thought of sharing it with Tyler made her practically giddy.

It must have showed, too. Natalie had asked her five times that morning if she’d had too much coffee. It had been all she could do to make it through until closing time.

Now she was on her way to Tyler’s house. He hadn’t called or come by today. For half a second she was reminded of times when she’d been a coltish fourteen, sitting on the steps of her house in the hope that Tyler would just happen to walk by. He almost never did, and she never could get up the nerve to say hello when it did happen, but still she had waited.

She wasn’t waiting anymore. She was…making a fool of herself.

‘‘No, I’m not,’’ she said to herself sternly, whipping into a turn. ‘‘He asked me to help him and I’m helping him. This is different. Besides, I’m too old to indulge in those kinds of girlish daydreams. Tyler and I are from different worlds, we want different things, and I'm going on a date with Darryl tonight. This is purely a business matter between Tyler and me."

She felt pretty darn smug thinking like that, at least until she pulled up in front of his house, which had turned even more beautiful practically overnight.

"Oh, my," she said as she exited her car and walked down the bricked path to the front door. Workmen were everywhere. Landscapers. Carpenters. She pushed open the door and went inside. The scent of paint and varnish and new-cut wood tickled her nose. Bright sunshine poured into the front parlor that was being papered in a cream-and-blue floral print from another time. The dark mahogany wood trim gleamed.

Her first inclination was to call Tyler's name, like a wife coming home to her husband, but she caught herself short. She was a visitor here, an outsider, as she'd always been.

"Excuse me," she said softly to a workman passing through. "Is Mr. Westlake on the premises?"

The man gave her a lopsided grin. "Tyler?" he asked.

At her nod he cupped a hand around his mouth. "Hey, Ty, there's a beauty here to see you. Do you want to take her question or shall I?" He gave Lilah a slow wink.

Lilah blinked her eyes. She heard a laugh and looked up to see Tyler, tall and strong and green-eyed, and coming down the staircase toward them.

"Stay away from my woman, Roger, or I'll have to fire you before you've finished the job."

Before Lilah could swivel her head in astonishment, Roger gave a hearty laugh. "Pay no mind to him, miss.

It's an old joke between Tyler and me. All the ladies in the world are divided into two camps. They're either 'his woman' or 'my woman,' whoever sees her first. Just a game we play on account of the first time Tyler came upon me, I was sixteen years old and attempting to protect a woman twenty years my senior from a gang of thugs by loudly proclaiming that they had better stay away from 'my woman.' Tyler backed me up with his fists and his money, helped the woman find shelter and helped me find medical attention after one of the thugs took a swing at me. It's just a bit of nostalgia, nothing that would mean any disrespect, you understand, my darlin'?''

Lilah couldn't help laughing at the man's sorrowful, polite tone and his slight Irish accent, which appeared to be affected.

''He's full of nonsense, Lilah. Don't listen to the scoundrel,'' Tyler said with a grin. ''I wouldn't even hire him except he's a master with a bit of wood. Lilah Austin, meet Roger Quinlan.''

The man held out a hand and gave her a big smile. ''Ah, so you're Ms. Austin. I've heard you're the heartbreaker from the bookstore.''

Roger Quinlan must be full of mischief and tall tales if he claimed to have heard she was a heartbreaker, but she was pretty sure his tale of how he and Tyler met was straight out of the book of truth. She shook his hand gladly.

''Pleased to meet you, Mr. Quinlan, although I don't think I've broken any hearts lately. I just sell books, and I've just come by to talk to Tyler about something regarding his house.''

Immediately the man held a hand over his heart. ''Ah, you're wrong, then, Ms. Austin. You've broken my heart if that's all you've come for. I've lost out to Tyler and his blasted green eyes again."

Tyler had moved to the bottom of the steps and clapped his shorter friend on the back. "You've brought tears to my eyes, Roger. I'm dreadfully sorry to have to steal Lilah from you, but she's mine, you see. All mine. Come on, angel," he told her, holding out his hand.

And charming though Roger Quinlan was, Lilah placed her hand eagerly in Tyler's. She smiled up into his stunning dark-green eyes and followed him back up the stairs to a small study on the second floor.

When he pulled a chair out at a desk and motioned for her to sit down, she looked around at the room, which had been dark and cramped only a brief week ago. It was clean and bright now, all done up in cream silk and rose trappings, the cherrywood desk catching the gleam of sunlight coming in through the windows.

"How did you do so much so fast?" she asked, staring at the exquisite furnishings.

He shrugged. "Manpower. Lots of manpower. The rest is easy. For a price furniture and paint, even period furnishings and wallpaper can be had if one only knows who to ask and what to ask for. It's what I've specialized in, so I know who to talk to and what to ask for. I've just decided—well, let's just say I'm hoping—to speed up production here and finish this quickly."

He was staring directly at her now, but his eyes gave nothing away.

"You have somewhere else you have to be?" She regretted the distress in her voice the minute the words had left her mouth.

Tyler moved closer, then backed off a step. Finally he gave a slight smile and held out his hands palms up. "Wouldn't be fair to my brother to take any longer on it than necessary. He and his wife would like to move in and get started as soon as possible."

Of course. He hadn't come here to vacation this time, and helping her had probably thrown his schedule off a tad. She wanted to tell him once again that he didn't need to help her anymore. Indeed, the more time she spent with him the more distressing were the things that happened. Like that kiss the other night or the way she kept seeing his smile in her dreams or the way she was beginning to compare other men to him. All foolishness, all impractical, and over the years as a businesswoman she'd learned how to court the practical and curb the dreamer in herself.

"You need to conclude your business as soon as possible. Of course," she said quietly. "I—well, I brought you something that pertains to your business. Something I found last night." She rose and removed a small red book from the portfolio she'd been carrying. A page was marked with a strip of red ribbon.

He took the book from her, read the section she'd marked and smiled. "Where on earth did you find this?"

Lilah shrugged. "I have a thing about old diaries. This one happened to belong to a local woman who was apparently thrown into a rare tizzy at the thought of being given the honor of entertaining the Westlakes. Even back then your family was thought of as royalty in Sloane's Cove."

"So she spent three weeks trying to decide which one of my great grandmother's favorite foods she would put in a cake. Coconut, walnuts or chocolate. I wonder what she chose."

"Oh, she chose chocolate. A pudding of some sort,

I believe. I have the other entries, which I've saved for you. I understand your grandmother declared the dish to be 'tolerable,' which was considered quite a compliment by the woman. I thought you might want the diary entries to display, and I've saved the book for you.''

''You're a treasure, Lilah. I couldn't just take one of your beloved diaries, though.''

She raised her chin. ''Uh-oh. You're not going to insult me by suggesting you reimburse me for it, are you? It's mine to have and mine to give if I want to. You think I'd take money from you after you've given so much time and attention to help me find a husband of my own?''

He sucked in a deep breath. ''I rather thought the problem was that you had too *many* men wanting you.''

She fought her urge to lean closer at the low, deep tone of his voice. He knew perfectly well what her situation had been and what it was now. It was only in the past few days that men had begun wondering if there was something that lay beneath the surface of the woman they'd always known. It was Tyler's pretended interest that had made them wake up and wonder. He could belittle his participation, but she never would.

''I want you to have the diary,'' she insisted, ''and this, too, if you're interested.'' She pulled a beautiful sheet of cream vellum from her folder. On it had been printed a recipe for a dark-chocolate, coconut cake with walnut cream filling.

''What's this?''

She felt a blush coming on. ''I had my sister make it up. It's a recipe just for your restaurant. Helena's a great cook. The best.'' The absolute best since she'd been able to come up with this in only one evening. "I just thought you should have something that was...unique for your unique and very beautiful restaurant. Since I assume we won't be seeing much of each other from now on—I mean, you've already fulfilled your end of the bargain—I thought I would give you this now. As a thank-you for your help."

She couldn't keep staring into those green eyes. The urge to move close was too intense, the need to kiss him again was too frighteningly real. Lilah looked down at the portfolio she was carrying.

"Lilah." His very voice was a caress. Tyler slid long fingers beneath her jaw. He tipped her head up to look at him. Silently he bent and touched his lips to hers. Just the slightest of touches.

She felt as if he'd set fire to her soul. Hunger more intense than anything she'd ever experienced flowed through her.

"Thank you," he whispered, and he kissed her again. "I know your sister's reputation. She's a legend in her field. This is most special. Like you, Lilah."

She opened her lips beneath his, and for one brief moment he caught her to him. Then, just as quickly, he froze, released her and backed away.

"Thank you," he said again, and for a moment she thought he was thanking her for the kiss. Of course she quickly realized she was wrong. Tyler had kissed hundreds of women. She was pretty sure it was the women who were grateful, not the other way around.

"I guess—I guess I'd better be going," she said to hide her sudden discomposure.

"Oh, yes, it's Friday. You have a date to get ready for," he said, as if he'd just remembered. "What are you wearing?"

She hadn't decided. She hadn't even thought that much about her date with Darryl, a fact that made her feel more than a little guilty, since she'd spent a lot of time thinking about Tyler.

Shrugging, she shook her head. ''Clothing?''

''Great idea. I'll be there at six. You can show me. I know a lot about women's clothing.''

And with that he kissed her again, stroked one finger down her cheek and turned her around, nudging her toward the stairs. It was only after he'd walked her to her car, put her inside, shut the door and made sure she was safely on her way that Lilah's brain kicked back into action.

She was going on a date tonight, and Tyler Westlake was going to help her get dressed. There was just something very wrong with that picture.

Chapter Nine

When Lilah came out of her bedroom that night, Tyler felt a bittersweet swirl of ''oh, no'' rush through him. Dressed in rose-pink, her taffy-colored hair long and silky where it lay against her shoulders, she was achingly beautiful, too beautiful for any man, even a ''good'' man such as Darryl.

''How—that is—is this okay?'' she asked hastily, looking down at the wide belt of her linen dress. The slender skirt hit below the knee, emphasizing the lovely curves of her legs. The bright color of the dress complemented her pale skin perfectly.

Tyler nodded approvingly. ''It's perfect. You're exquisite,'' he said, the words thick in his throat as she came toward him. ''Just one small change.''

She looked up, a question in those meltingly pretty eyes.

''Nothing wrong with you,'' he said quietly. ''Let's just do this, though.''

He reached out and fastened the top button on the front of the collared dress, the one that was usually meant to remain open. He cupped her jaw with his hand and gently stroked his thumb across her lip, smudging off a hint of rose-pink lipstick in an attempt to make her lips less kissable. As if anything could do that.

Lilah traced a finger over the restricting, buttoned neckline and raised one brow.

"He's not going to jump me, Tyler."

"If he does that, he dies at dawn."

She gave a laugh, and he realized that she thought he was teasing. Well, maybe he was, but the sentiment still held. He would personally join forces with the Austin brothers if Darryl Hoyne stepped over the line.

As it was, he just stood gazing down at her, trying to see her the way a man might if it was their first date. Her lips were parted slightly, her eyes luminous. If he were Darryl, he'd be thinking of seeing what he could do to make those eyes grow passionate. He'd be wondering what it would be like to nibble on those lips and get them to open wider.

Tyler dragged in a deep breath. He shoved one hand back through his hair.

Lilah was looking a trifle uncertain, as if she knew what he'd been thinking. Had he leaned too close? Had he stared at her mouth too long? Was he starting to act like a schoolboy who'd never kissed a woman before? No doubt about that.

"I should go," he offered, but he didn't budge.

She stared up at him, then nodded tightly. "Darryl's kind of shy. He might find the sight of you a bit intimidating."

Tyler managed a slight smile. Shy was good.

''Enjoy your evening, sweetheart,'' he whispered, and he swung out the door and away.

An hour and a half later he realized he'd been staring at the same page of a book for ten minutes. His mind had been nowhere near the history of Maine. It had been in the present, right in the theater, planted solidly beside Lilah and her date. He hoped Darryl was keeping his hands where they belonged. Right in the popcorn box.

''Hell, get a grip, Westlake. She's not your responsibility.'' But he glanced at his watch once again. Finally he threw down the book, strode down the stairs and climbed into his car.

Lilah wouldn't thank him for doing this, but he was doing it, anyway. Driving to her house. Half a block away he parked. He waited. And waited.

Damn. The movie should have let out half an hour ago. Maybe even forty-five minutes. Where in hell were they? The possibilities were…something he didn't even want to think about.

Finally, ten minutes later, he heard the sound of a car. Something big. Seconds later Darryl pulled his sport utility up in front of Lilah's house. A few seconds passed. A few seconds more. Then Lilah climbed out. She waved good-night and moved toward her stairs as her date drove away.

Anger, sharp and irritating, nudged at Tyler. She was still on the stairs, still in the dark, and the man hadn't even waited to see that she was safely inside.

''He's a swine, love,'' Tyler whispered, still in his

car, "if he didn't even walk you to the door and see that you were protected."

Tyler waited. He watched Lilah locate her keys and let herself inside the house. The light flickered on inside. Only then did he leave. He drank in the first real breath of relief he'd breathed all night. Even though he knew there was trouble ahead. A man just didn't tell a woman who to date.

On his way back down the street, Tyler passed Bill Austin. The man looked at him, smiled slightly, then turned his car around and headed for home.

Tyler had been caught spying on Lilah. He was no better than her brothers. Funny, but he didn't feel even the least bit apologetic about it.

That woman could drive men to do things they wouldn't have done ordinarily. That was just all there was to it. Tomorrow she'd know it, too, because he was going to talk to her about Darryl. He'd promised to help Lilah find her man, but there was no way in hell he was going to hand her over to the wrong man.

"You'd think it was Christmas," Lilah mumbled beneath her breath as she slipped into the storage room to grab a couple of minutes of solitude from the bookstore crowd the next morning.

For hours people had been coming in, looking at her expectantly, smiling. As if she were going to do a play-by-play of her date last night.

Not that it wouldn't have been perfectly acceptable to do so. Darryl was a very nice man. The evening had gone well. The movie had been pleasant. And then the night had ended. Nothing exciting. No sharing of confidences, no unexpected occurrences, just a nice movie and a nice man. If she'd looked at him and wondered why her heart didn't race, if she'd wished his eyes made her stomach flip over, that was just silliness on her part. The kind of reactions that only happened in books.

Even though she'd met a man who did those very things to her.

"Wrong man," she said sternly. And this was the wrong time to be thinking about Tyler. She had customers who needed attention, and in a few weeks she'd still have customers. Tyler, on the other hand, would be out of her life very quickly. Men like Darryl were her reality. She had better learn to like simply feeling friendly if that was all there was to be.

Lilah took a deep breath. She shoved out the storage room door and waded into the crowd again.

"Lilah, babe, you've got some great stuff here," Joe Rollins said, holding out a history of the harem. "I think you and I need to get together and talk books real soon."

She smiled weakly and moved on.

"Lilah, about lunch. We really do need to get together and talk finances," Avery told her. "I know this great little place in Ellsworth that has quiet booths. How about—" he pulled out a planner and flipped through the pages "—how about a week from Thursday? I'll bring the wine. You bring the beauty."

She wanted to laugh at the fact that he had scheduled her in like a client, and yet it wasn't funny. Avery was nice. He was a busy man, and he meant well. He was the kind of man she should be seriously considering for her own.

Lilah took a deep breath. She forced herself to open her mouth. ''That would be very nice, Avery.''

A long, leggy blond woman winked at Avery, and he blushed and dropped his planner. The woman leaned over toward Lilah. ''Hey, hon, you wouldn't happen to know if Tyler is coming into town today, would you? I've got a thing about that man, and now that you're out of the picture, well…''

Immediately Lilah felt the crush of people closing in, and she knew that something was very wrong. She ordinarily loved it when her bookstore hummed. She adored the banter with customers, but this wasn't the usual banter.

''I'm sorry, I don't know where Tyler is or if he's coming here,'' Lilah told the woman, who gave her a satisfied smile.

''Good. Just checking. I'll go look for him elsewhere. My vacation's almost up and there's no time to lose with that one. Have to grab those lips while you can.''

She was definitely right about that. Maybe Tyler would disappear from her life now that men were pursuing her. That was the way it should be, so why did she want to make excuses to keep him near?

Because she was no better than any of these other women, Lilah admitted with a frown.

''Lilah?'' Philip Eddison, who worked in the chamber of commerce offices, leaned close and jolted her back into the world of the bookstore.

She looked up at him. ''I—hello. May I help you, Phil?''

He smiled. ''You look harried. Can't say as I blame you. You've created quite a stir around here. Too many men?''

Not exactly.

''You can't blame them, you know,'' he said quietly. ''You always seemed kind of poetic and unattainable, too saintly to be real. Now everyone sees that you're genuine flesh and blood, and most of the men around here have a taste for flesh and blood. Me included.''

She blinked and tried to adjust her thinking. Phil had pulled her pigtails when she'd been eight years old. He'd taught her her first bad word and gotten her in trouble.

''Don't worry,'' he said with a laugh and a wink. ''I'll wait until the excitement dies down to ask you out. Maybe I'll teach you a few dirty words again. Get you in trouble with all the old biddies. Maybe even a few tricks Westlake doesn't know or hasn't shown you yet.''

Lilah's eyes widened as she realized that Phil Eddison was propositioning her.

The incongruity of that lifted her spirits a little and she smiled. ''Shame on you, Phil,'' she drawled. ''If you don't behave yourself, I'll finally tell your mother that you were the one who taught me all I know about swearing, and she'll rip your ear off.''

He grinned and shrugged. ''Well, it was worth a try. Sure you don't want to get naked with me?''

His timing couldn't have been more off. The lull in conversation that his question fell into was absolutely perfect. The whole mass of customers seemed to turn as one and stare at the two of them. The quiet was so complete that Lilah could hear the cuckoo-clock bell sounding in a store two doors down.

Into this silence Tyler entered, with the blond woman close on his heels.

A brunette beauty sauntered forward, peering testily at the blonde. ''Well, Tyler, you've come just in time for all the fun. This man here,'' she said, pointing to Phil, ''has just asked your friend to get naked with him. Isn't that adorable?''

The crowd seemed to gasp in unison. Phil choked on a laugh. Lilah rolled her eyes skyward. The brunette and the blonde squared off, eyeing each other. To Lilah's amusement Phil looked interested in the ensuing battle between Tyler's ladies.

Tyler, however, looked less than amused. He was smiling slightly, but his eyes—his eyes were dark and fierce and blazing.

''Excuse us, will you, Natalie?'' he said. ''Lilah, I have a question about the house I'd like to ask you. You're the only one who can help me, I'm afraid.''

He held out his hand.

She'd be a fool to take that hand, Lilah thought. If she put her palm against his, she knew what she would feel. She'd felt it before. Passion. Longing. Pain swelled up from within her as she reminded herself that Tyler was interested in her only as a friend. He was becoming more like her brothers every day, interested in her welfare the way one would care for a child's welfare.

''Maybe I should take Phil up on his offer,'' she

muttered as she placed her hand in his and followed him out the door.

He carefully led her toward his car, and she allowed him to. He tucked her inside and she allowed that, also.

But when he'd driven down the road and pulled over on a deserted stretch of highway and turned to her, she held up her hand.

''Do not lecture me about Phil Eddison. He didn't mean a thing by his comment. That's just Phil. Tomorrow he'll be asking some other woman to get naked with him. Maybe even today. It doesn't mean anything. He's actually pretty harmless.''

Tyler gave her a sideways glance. ''So, does this mean you're going to take him up on his offer?''

His brow was raised the way it would be if he were teasing her, but his look was still intense. She wanted him to smile at her. For some reason it seemed very important that he smile at her right now. Lilah wondered if she was becoming like those other women, the ones who had given up their vacations to chase after Tyler. She also wondered if Tyler would have sampled those women if he hadn't been baby-sitting her.

A protest rose up inside her. She squelched it. It would only hurt Tyler and make him feel guilty to think that in trying to help her, he'd succeeded in making her want things he could never give. She needed to move the mood back to a lighter plane.

''Hmm, am I going to take Phil up on his offer of getting naked?'' she asked, as if she were actually considering the matter. ''Well, Tyler, let me put it this way. Phil is sweet, but he can't keep a secret at all. Do you think I want everyone in town talking about the tattoo I have on my inner thigh?''

Tyler blinked. His eyes turned darker, narrower, if that were possible. He leaned closer.

''You have a tattoo on your inner thigh?''

She shook her head and smiled, reaching out to stroke her palm down his jaw. ''No, but if I did, Phil would tell. I think I'll pass on this offer of his.''

''What if he offered something else, something more substantial than climbing into his bed? Frankly, the guy looked slightly smitten.''

''I've known him all my life.''

''He's seeing you in a new light.''

She nodded. ''That's something I'll have to think about. Phil really is a sweet man, Tyler. In time he might make someone a good husband. And in spite of his tendency to tease and to kiss and tell, I'm not afraid of him. He's a friend.''

Tyler groaned and turned his jaw deeper into her palm. ''Trust me, Lilah. I know men like him. I *am* a man like him. He's not right for you. I think our plan may have been a bad idea.''

Her breath froze in her throat. ''You're sorry for helping me?'' For the times we've spent together, she wanted to say.

''If I'd helped you, I wouldn't be sorry, but if I've hurt you or brought grief into your life...Lilah, I've made a lot of mistakes in my life. I'm no good at relationships. My wife told me so, and she was right. I'm not the best man to engineer matters of the heart.''

''You haven't hurt me.''

''Darryl didn't even walk you to your door last night.''

She opened her eyes wide. She pulled her hand away from the seductive sensation of holding it against the rough plane of his jaw.

Tyler blew out a breath. ''Someone needed to make sure you got home safely.''

She had to smile at that, even though she shook her head.

''Darryl didn't do anything wrong, Tyler.''

''He should have been a gentleman.''

''He was.''

''A gentleman walks a woman to her door.'' She could almost hear his mother's voice drilling the lesson into him.

''This is Sloane's Cove. What could happen?''

He let out a long breath, ran one finger across her lower lip. ''You're such an innocent, Lilah.''

''I'm not. I'm a realist.''

''Are you going out with him again?'' Tyler's words were sharp, clipped.

''Probably not. We're just friends. I'm going out with Avery, though.''

''The banker.''

''Yes, he found an empty slot in his schedule for us to have lunch.''

''You deserve more.''

She shook her head. ''Don't worry, Tyler. Avery is—''

''I know. Avery is a good man.''

''He is.''

''He's not good enough. You can do better.''

But she laughed. She'd always considered herself a dreamer, but now she knew that Tyler was an even bigger dreamer. She hadn't wanted much, just a nice man who would love her. Right now she didn't feel anything special toward Darryl or Avery or Phil. But maybe she would in time. She hoped so.

She wanted to be seriously considering a husband by the time Tyler left town and, judging by the way his work was progressing, he might very well vanish as quickly as he had the last time. Under no circumstances did she want to be missing him once he had gone. She needed to settle on a potential fiancé fast. It was time to make some decisions.

''You can see that not one of those guys deserves her.'' Tyler finished his speech and looked at the woman who looked so much like Lilah and at the same time so very different.

''Whoa,'' Helena said. ''It's really fun hearing this story from ten different perspectives. You're not the first to tell me what's been going on in Lilah's store, you know. My sister seems to have set the town on its ear, hasn't she?''

''I don't want to see Lilah giving her heart to the wrong kind of man,'' Tyler said, pacing to the window. He turned around and stared back at Helena.

She smiled.

''What?''

''Nothing. I just think it's…interesting that a man who's known as the town's greatest playboy is worried about Lilah getting involved with the wrong kind of man.''

"Maybe I know a lot more about that kind of man than the average male."

"Maybe you do."

"Will you help?" he asked. "I've told her what I think, that neither Avery nor Phil qualifies as the right kind of man for her, but she just keeps insisting that these men are very nice friends of hers."

"And they are. Lilah doesn't lie."

"I know she doesn't. She's honest and sincere and way too giving and trusting. She could have any man. But he has to be the *right* kind of man," he said, his voice clipped and precise. It was his business voice, and he felt a little guilty using it on Lilah's sister, because he knew he could be intimidating at such times, but the situation was serious. She needed to know that.

"Will you help?" he asked. "Talk to her?"

"I could do that," she said softly, "but it wouldn't do any good. Lilah and I are close, but…growing up as twins, we both had to develop our own independence or risk being lumped together all the time. Lilah seems soft and, yes, she's easily hurt, but she has a stubborn streak that people overlook at times. She takes a long time to make up her mind, but once it's made up, she's unswerving, ever faithful. If she's decided that these 'good men' deserve her attention, she'll give it to them."

"She could have more," he insisted.

"Maybe she doesn't know what 'more' looks like. This is a small town. We all become a bit familiar with each other. We take each other for granted, so some of the niceties fall by the wayside at times. If you want her to have the right kind of man, maybe you should show her what the right kind of man would be like.''

''The last time I tried to show anyone anything, Lilah and I were pretending to be lovers, and that's what brought all of these snakes crawling up her driveway.''

''So show them something else. Show Lilah. I *am* on your side, you know. I want what's best for her. And I agree, Phil is great fun, but he'd make her completely miserable. That's not acceptable.''

Tyler gazed into eyes of a different blue than Lilah's and realized he had an ally here. A worried ally.

''No one is going to make Lilah miserable,'' he declared.

''I'm glad to hear that. What are you going to do?''

He breathed out a sigh. ''It seems I'm going to do my best to show Lilah what she should be looking for in a man. I'm going to attempt to transform myself, temporarily, into the perfect suitor.''

Chapter Ten

Lilah had barely arrived home the next evening when her doorbell rang. She opened the door and found Tyler standing there. He was holding a small bouquet of pink rosebuds. His smile was slow and…friendly.

Immediately Lilah wondered what was wrong. When Tyler looked at a woman, "friendship" was not the woman's first thought. Those green eyes could be amused, interested, even angry, but they always reminded a woman of passion. Today he looked merely happy to see her. The way an old friend might.

"I thought you might consider going to dinner with me if you were free," he said, extending the bouquet. "I'd be honored if you would."

Rivulets of heat rose within her. She glanced up shyly from beneath her lashes. For a minute, she thought she detected a trace of the raw sexuality that had characterized Tyler for as long as she'd known him, but then she blinked and decided she'd made a mistake. He was still smiling, his brow raised, as he waited for her response.

She took the bouquet. "Thank you. Yes, I'd like that."

"I thought I might ask you to read to me. You have such a compelling voice. I remember," he said. "Who wouldn't remember once he'd heard you read?"

"Tyler, are you all right?" she asked, reaching out to touch his forehead.

"A man can't compliment you on your voice?"

"Of course, and I'm grateful, but...there's something about you today. Something different."

"Maybe I'm just taking the time to enjoy our friendship. We've both been rather busy these past few weeks."

She nodded. "Yes, of course. I'll just go change."

He reached out to touch her arm, then pulled back. Slowly he shook his head. "Don't. Please. You're lovely as you are."

He held out his arm. It was a gallant gesture, reminiscent of stories she'd read in hundreds of books. She imagined that Tyler had done this same thing many times, but the funny thing was that she couldn't remember him holding his arm out to her before. He'd always taken her hand. Sometimes he'd even put his hand around her waist.

But then, they'd been putting on a show, she reminded herself. They weren't anymore. Now they were just...friends.

"I'll get a book," she promised, but he pulled one out of his jacket pocket and she nodded and took his arm. All right, then. They would go together as friends tonight. They would eat and read. This would be better than it had been. At last she could relax with Tyler.

Two hours later she was amending that thought. Relaxing was the last thing on her mind. Tyler was behaving himself perfectly. No dark, intense looks. No fingers stroking her cheek in a caress. His mouth never got near hers.

She was a wreck.

''Read one more paragraph,'' he urged, ''and then I'll give your voice a rest. It's just such a pleasure to hear you.''

He lounged back in his chair, toying with the stem of his wineglass. She remembered a day when he had sipped wine from her lips.

Lilah took a deep breath. ''The flowers of the field envied her,'' she began, her voice slightly raspy from her thoughts. She cleared her throat. ''The daffodils and tulips wore cloaks of yellow and white. Lovely, so lovely, but none lovelier than her.''

She stopped suddenly with a frown. ''Are you sure this is your kind of book, Tyler?''

He sat up straighter. ''Why do you ask?''

Finally he was looking slightly perturbed, that polished expression fading just a bit. She smiled to see a trace of the Tyler she knew.

''Well,'' she began, ''I spend most of my time with books, you know. I've gotten to be pretty good over the years about matching people to material, and I do have readers who prefer this style. This just doesn't seem to fit you.''

His smile grew. ''What would you suggest for me? Give me all your expertise, Lilah.'' A shade of that old sexiness had crept in. She glanced up into his eyes, but he blinked and all traces of sensuality were gone, replaced by simple curiosity.

''For you?'' she asked. ''Something laced with history, definitely. If we're talking fiction, something with sailing ships and adventure, with a touch of humor thrown in.''

He nodded. ''You're right. You know your customers very well, Lilah. You're a master at your business. I chose this mostly because the descriptions reminded me of you, and because I thought it would be a fitting background for this restaurant and the soft tones of your voice. It is, but I didn't mean to insult you. I'd never do that. I respect you far too much.''

''I respect you, too,'' she said with a smile. ''Has a woman ever told you that?''

He laughed. ''Never. And now that we're both respecting each other so much, I'll take you home. You've been busy the last few days. You need your rest.''

A small sense of disappointment made her want to protest, but she couldn't. He had appeared out of nowhere, with flowers and literature and an offer of a meal with a friend. How could she be less gracious?

She couldn't. But she wanted to.

More than that, what she really wanted to do was to press her lips to his and see if she could surprise the sensual man she'd grown to know into showing up again.

But that wouldn't be fair. The game was over. She had gotten to be wild and dangerous for a few days, but now she was just simple Lilah Austin again.

Someday soon she'd settle on a nice, quiet man who liked her for her and they'd set about making a future. It would be a simple future, nothing wild and dangerous about it.

And she would be happy. She swore she would. It was what she'd wished for, after all, wasn't it?

* * *

This was far more difficult than he'd ever imagined it would be, Tyler thought as he prepared to take Lilah out again two days later. He wasn't used to being the perfect suitor. He wasn't used to being a suitor at all, even a pretend one, and quiet, sweet Lilah Austin didn't make him feel polite and charming. She made him feel like a volcano on the verge of erupting. Trying to pretend otherwise was consuming great reserves of his energy. Tonight he was going all-out to convince her to wait until the right man came along. He was going to put his all into this performance.

He hoped it worked. Her date with the banker was coming up soon. Tonight he would show Lilah and everyone else in Sloane's Cove what she had every right to expect from a man, and then he was going to have to think about leaving. If he had to, he would bring in one of his siblings to finish this job. It was something he'd never done before, but then he'd never behaved this way with a woman before, either. It was time to get back to the old ways. Spend a few weeks at the island, then leave. He would put her out of his mind. She would move on.

The thought of her marrying, having another man's babies, growing old with the man she would eventually choose sliced his breath away. Not that it mattered. He wanted her, but he couldn't have her.

''And what if I'm gone and old Avery convinces her to settle for a life of concessions?'' he whispered.

That was not going to happen. Not if he did this right. By the end of the evening, she would know what she could and should expect from a man. Respect, admiration, adoration, with just a hint of passion to come. Thank goodness he only had to pretend for one night.

Any more than that and he'd be no better than Phil Eddison, trying to entice her into his bed.

The thought made him see red…and hot-white. He threw the car into a parking space in front of her house, strode up the steps and rapped on her door just a bit too hard in his attempt to keep ahead of his thoughts.

Lilah came to the door dressed in a pale-blue dress with a V-neck that drew a man's attention downward. Tyler forced himself to concentrate on her eyes. He reached into his pocket and withdrew a scarf.

"Good evening, sunshine," he said. "Are you ready for a surprise tonight?"

She smiled. "You've finished more of the house?"

"We've finished a fair amount, but that's not what this is about."

Lilah shook her head. "Then you've located some historic sloop you want to transform."

"Umm, that's probably a plan I'm going to have to drop."

"Then what's the surprise?"

"Nothing special. Just a night with you in mind." He held out the scarf. "I thought maybe we'd have an evening created just for the reader in you."

She grinned and leaned forward peering at the scarf. "Is there writing on that?"

"No, there's magic here, though." And he held out the scarf. "You see," he said, his voice low. "I was just thinking about how, as a businesswoman, you spend so much time reading people's expressions. You watch them and read their reactions and go out of your way to make people happy. But this isn't work tonight, and this evening is supposed to be all about you. For you. If you can't see what I'm thinking, you'll rely on all those other senses you've honed so well in your years as a reader.'' Besides, if he couldn't see her eyes, maybe he wouldn't be so damned tempted by the woman.

He held out the scarf.

Lilah widened her eyes. ''I'm not exactly sure about this.''

''It *does* carry an element of risk, I'll grant you that,'' he said. ''You'd have to trust me to allow me to blindfold you.''

She nodded then and stepped forward.

He wanted to swear. Like that she came to him. Didn't she know that it was taking all his self-control not to ask her to make love with him? That under any other circumstances he'd be doing his best to steal her innocence away from her?

''I trust you,'' she said, staring resolutely up at him, and those blue eyes nearly slayed him.

He covered them gently with the scarf.

''Tonight is just for you,'' he said to her, but it was himself he was actually reminding.

Gently, he placed her hand on his sleeve and led her down the stairs and into his car. He drove out into the night to Sea Watch. There he led her to a table set up beneath the trees. The ocean lay nearly at their feet, the mountains of the island behind them, but of course, Lilah couldn't see any of that.

''Where are we?'' he asked.

Lilah raised her face and breathed in. ''We're near the water. I can smell the salt and feel the ocean breeze. I can hear the waves lapping against the shore.'' Then her smiled deepened. ''And I can definitely hear a small sound of hammering. We must be at your mother's home.''

He grinned at that. ''You are amazing, Lilah. We

are at Sea Watch, but we're actually quite a distance from the house. The sound of that hammering is barely discernible even to me and I already knew it was there.''

She laughed. ''I've spent a great deal of time in my storage room, keeping an ear out for customers. Besides, I live alone. The creaking of the boards in my house is sometimes the only conversation I hear at night.''

But what Lilah was hearing right now were her own doubts. Why was Tyler still being so solicitous of her? Not that he hadn't been since the very first time she'd come across him this summer. But then they'd had a bargain. Now she had men appearing at her door just for her, not because her brothers had sent them. Tyler had accomplished his mission. There was no reason for him to be wining and dining her now. Not when he could have many of the myriad women who kept appearing in her bookstore searching for him. The thought made her frown.

She reached up to remove her blindfold.

''Not yet,'' he said, and she paused. It occurred to her that in more recent days he would have stopped her with a touch, not just words.

But that was yesterday, and today was something different. They were just friends now, no longer co-conspirators in a mad, passionate, exciting charade.

Life had settled down.

Too soon he'd be gone, Lilah thought, like before. She remembered past summers, how she'd felt the first time she'd seen him, with his long, lean form, his killer smile and the way he tended to his mother even when the woman chided him. She remembered his politeness, his gallantry. He had seemed lonely in those days. Something in him had called to her.

It still did, only the feeling was much more intense now.

The admission stabbed at her, but there was no point in following that line of thought. Tyler wasn't a lonely man. He had women at his beck and call. He was successful. Satisfied. It was only the romantic in her that had dared to even imagine something in his soul had once called out to hers. Besides, dwelling on dreams about Tyler could only lead to heartbreak, because to love a Westlake was to lose at love.

It was as if a blinking neon sign flashed before her. She *was* already falling in love with Tyler. But surely it wasn't too late to do the sensible thing and stop.

She would marry someone from home. He would go back to the life he'd chosen, a life of freedom and passion.

Lilah thinned her lips at the thought, but she pursued it.

"What's wrong?" Tyler asked, but there was no way she could tell him. He would feel guilty. He already felt that he'd failed his wife. No way would she let him think he had failed her in any way. He hadn't.

"Nothing's wrong. I'm just...sniffing," she said with an attempt at a smile. "Are you going to feed me? I thought I smelled food."

"Lilah," he drawled, "do you really believe that I would leave you hungry? Never. The Westlakes are in the restaurant business, and besides, I've just brought in a new chef. Be prepared. Sit back and relax, my dear Ms. Austin."

Lilah sat back. She felt a bit grumpy at being called

Ms. Austin when she'd grown used to "sweetheart" and "angel," but thinking that way was unreasonable.

In a moment she heard Tyler rise from his seat. There was a hushed whoosh, and then the soft strains of Pachelbel's "Canon" filtered into the night, mingling with the chorus of waves and seagulls. She heard the click of a match, breathed in the slight smell of sulfur and the comforting scent of vanilla.

"Rest," he urged. "You've had a longer-than-usual week with all the comings and goings at your store. You need some time to unwind. I want you to have as much time as you need. Your needs are what's important, Lilah. Just yours."

His low voice soothed, and she wished he'd come closer, but he didn't. When the muffled thud of footsteps on grass reached her, followed by the ring of china against china, Lilah sat up straighter. The scent of thyme and basil drifted to her.

Tyler thanked whoever had brought their food.

"Will you mind if I feed you?" he asked after their server had gone.

Her throat suddenly felt tight. "I…I suppose that would be all right."

He chuckled. "You don't sound at all sure of that. Trust me, Lilah."

She did, so she let him feed her. Gently he nudged her lips with her fork. She parted her lips and for a second she thought she heard him breathe in more deeply, but she must have been mistaken because in the next second, he was speaking perfectly calmly.

"I'm not embarrassing you, am I?" he asked.

Lilah let the food melt in her mouth. She swallowed, she savored, she realized that if this were any other man, she would be embarrassed. She would also not be feeling this discontent. She shouldn't be feeling such frustration, but she couldn't help it. Tyler was feeding her senses, admirably so. She was feasting on sounds and smells and tastes, but…he hadn't touched her. Not really. It was as if he was deliberately keeping his hands from her.

With a sudden deep sense of distress, she realized how much she'd come to crave his hands upon her body and his lips moving over her own. She wanted him to touch her. Terribly. It was all she could do to hold herself still and keep from forcing him to brush against her.

"Lilah?" he asked. "*Am* I embarrassing you?" he asked again, and she realized that she hadn't answered his question.

She shook her head hard. "No," she said softly, trying to hide the aches and disappointments that were threatening to overcome her. She was losing him. She was distressed. He must not know that.

"You could never embarrass me," she said truthfully. "In fact, for someone who probably hasn't spent much time feeding other people, you're doing very well. You'd make someone a great mother."

He chuckled. "I'll keep that in mind and put it on my résumé."

"Tyler?"

"Yes?"

"Are you leaving soon?"

Silence stretched out.

"Yes, I think so," he finally said. "Why do you ask?"

"This feels a lot like goodbye."

"It does, doesn't it? I hadn't meant it to. We still have a little time."

The silence crept in; only the sounds of the waves on the rocks broke the quiet.

Then she felt his hand beneath her elbow. Very lightly he drew her to her feet, then immediately released her.

''Come,'' he said, placing her hand on his arm.

She followed him blindly, in a way she followed no one else.

They walked a ways, and she breathed in the scent of summer roses.

''The garden is finished,'' she said excitedly.

''Yes, almost everything will be finished soon.'' His words echoed her earlier comment. With the completion of the restaurant, she and Tyler would have also completed the strange and exhilarating relationship they'd shared this summer.

Gently she felt him slip the blindfold from her eyes. For a second the fading sunlight made her blink, but then the world came back into focus. Lilah looked around her, at the beauty of the mountains in the background, the sea close by, the flowers surrounding her and the man at her side.

Tyler wasn't looking at her. It was as if he was deliberately *not* looking at her. His concentration, instead, was on removing the thorns from the stem of a red rose he'd picked.

With a small, sad smile, he gave her a formal bow, then gently slipped the rose behind her ear.

''Let's go for a ride, my lady,'' he said, and as he moved aside, she noticed a carriage coming their way. A beautiful open black carriage pulled by a white horse. The driver pulled up and waited.

Tyler raised one brow and held out his hand to help

her inside. She laid her palm on his and immediately felt…safe.

"Where are we going?"

Tyler looked down at her. His mouth was smiling, but his eyes were dark and intense and unreadable.

"Just around the town. I'll have you home before the driver turns into a rodent," he promised.

And with the slightest of touches, he helped her climb up.

He joined her, seating himself a polite distance from her. They rode into town this way. She gazed at the lupines lining the fields and thought about how Tyler would be gone by August when the goldenrod was in such great glory and when the wild blueberries filled the crevices of even the most rugged mountaintop. She realized that she had wanted to take him to Bar Harbor at low tide when a person could walk the sandbar at the end of Bridge Street over to Bar Island. She wished that she could share with him the wonders of this place he'd summered at so long ago and realized that she could not.

And so she turned her attention completely to him. Tyler was an attentive escort. He asked her to relate the details of every landmark they passed. He listened, as if her every word were golden, but tonight was different from past nights. There were no endearments, no heated, intimate glances, no contact between her skin and his. He remained firmly on his side of the carriage. When they neared the town, he smiled down at her.

"It's beautiful here," he said. "It's fitting that you should live here. Like the cove, you're peaceful and lovely most of the time, a little wild and unpredictable some of the time. I hope the people of this town appreciate you, Lilah. You're quiet, but deep and observant. You pay attention to people, you care about them, and you deserve to be treated like a queen.''

''I'm that good, am I?'' she asked with a teasing look.

''Absolutely,'' he agreed. He never took his eyes off her, and she kept hers on him, but neither did he move nearer. Unlike their earlier public appearances, there was to be no touching whatsoever, and touching, Lilah was certain, came as naturally as smiling to Tyler.

A niggling suspicion came to her. From the moment Tyler had appeared in her bookstore, her brothers had tried their best to get her to steer clear of him. She should ask him if they'd been to see him lately, but would he tell her? He seemed to have this thing about protecting women. He wouldn't want to hurt her by criticizing her family.

So she said nothing. But she wondered. Tomorrow she'd pay a visit and find out what she wanted and needed to know.

For tonight Tyler was all she wanted to think about. He studied her every move it seemed, assessing her mood. His eyes never left hers, yet the carriage came to a stop in front of the flower shop.

She looked up at him quizzically. At this hour only a few shops were still open.

''Wait,'' he said with a smile, and suddenly the door of the shop opened. Mr. Trenton came out.

''Your young man knows your favorites,'' he said with a smile. ''So rare these days.'' He laid a tissue-wrapped bouquet into Lilah's arms. White, cultivated roses mingled with the wild pink roses that she'd picked in her youth. Yellow irises nestled in amongst them and the rich color of violets peeped out.

''How did you know?'' she asked Tyler.

He shook his head. ‘‘If a man decides to give a woman flowers, he should take the time to choose the right ones.’’

He looked at her pointedly and back to Mr. Trenton.

‘‘This is a man who knows how to court a woman,’’ Mr. Trenton pronounced as he moved back into his store.

Lilah breathed in the scent of the flowers. She looked up to find a small group of people watching…and listening.

Tyler signaled to the driver who moved on. The carriage traveled a block, the horses hooves clipping against the pavement, while a crowd of people hung out the windows and stopped on the sidewalks to watch. At the corner of Center and Birch, the carriage stopped once again. Tyler helped Lilah out of the carriage to a small table set up in front of the Mountain View restaurant. A waiter appeared with two cups.

‘‘Hot chocolate, not coffee,’’ he said, and Lilah raised one brow.

‘‘You've been talking to someone,’’ she said as she drew the cup toward her. Her suspicions were confirmed when Jeremy Flinn appeared, violin in hand and began to play something low and slow and stirring. She had a definite weakness for the violin. Once she'd even hoped to play herself, but that was a personal secret.

Tyler only gave her a noncommittal smile. ‘‘Some things are just to be enjoyed,’’ he insisted. ‘‘You should always have pleasure, Lilah. A person who wants to share your life should take the time to know you.’’

She looked up at him then, his voice so deep and intent. She rose to her feet and took a step closer.

For half a second she thought he would move to

meet her, but then he simply reached out and took her hand.

"It's late, my dear," he said. "A gentleman shouldn't keep a lady out when he knows she has to rise early the next morning."

Yet, he'd kept her out later before, she couldn't help thinking.

When there had been a purpose to those times together, she reminded herself. Now he was holding her at arm's length because there was no reason to do otherwise. He didn't want to kiss her the way she wanted him to kiss her, and that was all there was to it. Tonight he was being polite. He was acting as a friend, a summer neighbor. As he'd always been. Nothing closer. Their differences and the walls that separated them had never been clearer.

Lilah closed her eyes for a second to try to hold her emotions in check. She breathed long and slow, afraid he would see how painful this was, how much this evening was costing her.

When he escorted her back to her house, led her to the door and kissed her gently on the cheek, she felt her throat closing up.

"Be happy, Lilah," he said, his voice thick with worry. "I wish I could be certain that you'll be happy, that you'll be cared for once I'm gone." And then he opened her door for her, saw her inside and left. It occurred to her that soon he would be gone all the time.

Lilah moved deeper into the house. She closed the door. Mechanically she placed the flowers in water and got ready for bed, but sleep wouldn't come. She remembered her first day with Tyler, how fire had seemed to shoot between them from the beginning.

Tonight there had been charm, there had been elegance. Tyler had been the perfect escort, but he had not been the man she'd known. He had been a man who had courted her lavishly and then left her.

He had been both wonderful and ten times worse than any man she had known.

The insipidness of Darryl was preferable to having Tyler quoting sweet compliments to her while the fire in his eyes was banked, and while he moved farther and farther away from her.

He was on his way to leaving, so very politely, as her brothers had wanted him to from the first. Again, she couldn't help thinking that her brothers had had some part of this. Why else had her laughing, teasing, passionate Tyler disappeared so quickly and so thoroughly?

He didn't love her. She knew that. She'd always known he wouldn't, but this Tyler tonight, nice as he'd been, hadn't been the same man who'd come to town. He hadn't been the man she'd grown to love.

The man she'd grown to love. There it was again. The words stood out in her mind like a ten-foot title on a movie screen. No escaping the truth this time. No pretending she could stop loving him.

She wondered if it showed, if her brothers who read her so well had suspected and told Tyler. If they had, he would have felt guilty.

He might have felt a need to let her down easy. He might have started worrying over her, babying her.

Lilah realized with a jolt that that was exactly what Tyler had been doing, handling her with excessive care. Someone had made him feel guilty. That was unacceptable. It required action. No waiting, no hiding, no holding back.

Picking up her keys, she moved to the phone and called Hank.

"I want to talk to you and the others," she said quietly. "I'll be there in a few minutes."

Chapter Eleven

When she arrived, Bill and Hank and Thomas were already there. They lived within blocks of each other. Frank came in soon after, tucking his shirt in and brushing fingers through his tangled hair.

"This had better be good, Lilah," he warned.

"I never promised it would be, Frank."

"What's this all about, then?" Hank asked.

"I want to know what the four of you said to Tyler."

Bill raised one brow. "I assume you mean recently?"

"I suppose the question would be what did he say to you to bring this on?" Thomas added.

She shook her head. "Nothing about you."

"I hear he put on quite a show tonight," Frank said. "You didn't like it?"

"I'm human, Frank. I liked it, but…it was like I wasn't a woman. He didn't touch me once. Not really." She knew her eyes must be flashing sparks because Bill grinned.

"So you're mad because he didn't touch you, and you think we're to blame."

"Tyler always touches me."

"You want to explain that, little sister?" Hank demanded.

"No, I want you to tell me if you threatened him in some way. I want to know what you told him about me, what you revealed, what it was you saw in me that you mentioned to him. He was acting like..."

She studied her words.

"Like what?" Thomas asked softly.

"He was treating me like a queen," she said.

"I take it that's a bad thing," Frank said without much sympathy.

"It's a good thing," she admitted, "and the truth is, he always treats me with respect, but something was missing tonight. It was as if we were having a lesson. You know anything about that?"

All four brothers stood shoulder to shoulder. No one spoke. She looked up at them expectantly, hopefully.

"I suppose it wouldn't make any difference if I told you that I was in love with him."

Hank swore. Thomas slammed his fist into the wall.

"He doesn't love me back. He never encouraged me," she told them. "I didn't want him to know about it, either, but I thought maybe you'd guessed, that you'd told him. It would hurt him to know that. He wouldn't want to wound me. What did you say to him?"

Thomas shuffled his feet. "Lilah," he said, his voice filled with worry. "We didn't say anything to him, not for a long while, but—"

She lifted her chin, waiting.

"He went to see Helena," Frank said. "He didn't

think the men around here were treating you the way you deserved to be treated. I gather he decided to make you his personal quest, to demonstrate just how a woman like you deserved to be treated.''

Tears misted her eyes at his words. She didn't know why. To be so miserable because a man wanted something good for her just didn't make sense. After all, she and Tyler had been trying to influence the men of the town since he'd arrived. But this was different. He'd done this alone without consulting her. He'd known that men were beginning to ask her out, and he'd decided that those men weren't right for her, that he alone knew what type of man was ideal for her. It was this very kind of managing by her brothers that she'd been running from.

Besides, this turned their time last night into a mere performance, and not just for someone else, but for her. She'd thought she was a flesh-and-blood woman to him, but he'd treated her like a woman teetering on a pedestal, a hologram of the perfect virtues. She wouldn't be that for any man, especially not for Tyler, when she loved him so. Above all, she wanted to be real for him.

Not that he would ever love her back, but…darn it, the man had given up all his amusements for her these past few weeks so that she could have more from her life. He'd given up all, and in the end he'd allowed her to give up nothing, only to take.

That just wasn't right or fair to him. Didn't he deserve more than he'd gotten from life these past few weeks, too? Hadn't he given up all the women who were fainting over him? Weren't there women swarming around him, the kind she was sure he would have loved to be with if he hadn't been helping her?

There were. Tons of them. And if Tyler could decide what was best for her and work to ensure that she had those things, why shouldn't she do the same for him?

Lilah lifted her chin. She squared her shoulders. She began to turn ideas over in her mind.

"Thank you for leveling with me," she said coolly to her brothers.

"I don't like that look in your eyes, Lilah," Frank said.

"Don't like it, but don't get in my way, Frank."

"What are you going to do?" Bill asked.

"I'm going to see a man about a problem I have and to right a wrong that has been done. I'm going to do my darnedest to make a change."

"What kind of change?" Hank's voice was like a gunshot.

She leveled a long, cool look at him. "Watch," she said. "And see. I have a plan."

It wasn't much of a plan, she conceded as she drove away leaving four perturbed males behind, but it was the best she could do on short notice.

Tyler was a master at setting a scene, she admitted, remembering all the work he'd put into their last evening together. She would have to be just as good. When he left here, they would be even. She hoped he would leave happier than he'd been last night.

"I think I'll begin with something red...and tight," she said to herself. "Maybe something in black leather...and short, too," she added.

As soon as morning came, she'd call Helena, who was known to have a few wild things in her closet, and wild and exotic and shocking was exactly what Lilah was looking for.

Sometimes it took a sledgehammer to make a point with a man.

It was nine o'clock the next morning when Tyler's phone rang, and he was still in bed. Thinking, not sleeping. He'd hardly closed his eyes last night. All he'd been able to think about was the fact that he would be leaving Lilah soon. He had to go before she chose the man she wanted. It just wasn't possible for him to stay and watch her shine those smiles on another male. And if he had to watch Phil or Darryl or Avery tasting her lips, well—Tyler swore beneath his breath. He swung his legs out of bed, intending to escape his thoughts.

The phone was still ringing. He wanted to just let it lie, but his youngest stepbrother was planning to arrive in town to look over the progress of the restaurant today. It might be him. There might be a problem, and as the oldest Westlake, it was his responsibility to take care of the others.

He picked up the receiver.

''Tyler?'' Lilah's voice slipped over the lines, low and husky and incredibly sweet.

Tyler shoved his hand through his hair.

''Something's wrong,'' he said. She never called him.

For a second there was no sound on the line.

''Not exactly,'' she finally answered. ''But I need you to come meet me. I'll be waiting outside the store.''

''Angel—'' he began, but the line went dead.

''Hell,'' he said, grabbing for his pants. It was probably that Phil Eddison harassing her. If the woman couldn't even wait *inside* her store, then some jerk must have chased her out. Her store was her haven. There was no way he was going to let anyone mess with that or with her.

It crossed his mind that in just a few days he would be helpless to do anything at all to help Lilah, but he couldn't think about that right now. He was hell-bent on simply getting to her.

Skidding around corners, racing down straightaways, he flew through town, glad that it was still early and there were few people on the streets, but when he turned onto Main, he found out that he was wrong. There was a huge huddle of people in the middle of the block.

Right in front of Lilah's store.

Tyler threw the car in park, threw himself out of the car, and sprinted heart in throat toward the mass of people.

"Lilah," he yelled.

The crowd parted.

"I'm here, Tyler."

The voice was hers, soft and sexy. The eyes were hers, wide and blue. But the rest of the package was…not his Lilah.

Tyler drank in a deep gulp of air at the strapless, stretchy red tube that barely held in her breasts and exposed the creamy flesh of her stomach. His gaze dropped to a barely there black leather skirt that revealed yards of silky thigh. Two tiny strips of red leather and a pair of spiky heels were all there was of the shoes that raised her a good four inches and placed her breasts on a higher plane than usual.

A lot closer to some of the men's line of sight, too, he deduced, noting the way some of them were eyeing her.

"You want to tell me about it?" he asked slowly, edging out the people closest to him and removing his jacket at the same time.

"What are you doing?" she asked, as he shrugged out of his coat.

"I thought you might be cold, love," he whispered near her ear, holding out the jacket to cover as much of her as he could.

She tossed her head. "I'm not cold, Tyler. Not at all." Lilah's words weren't as low as his had been. A few people in the crowd chuckled.

Tyler cast a murderous look toward Joe Rollins, who appeared way too interested in the way Lilah's neck met her shoulder and curved into her breast.

Joe shrugged and grinned.

Tyler took a step closer to Lilah, although he was already standing next to her. He looked down into her eyes and at those lips she had painted a tantalizing shade of red. Her lips looked moist. As if she'd just licked them. While he stood there, staring, she did just that.

He couldn't keep himself from groaning.

Joe laughed out loud. Tyler shot him a take-your-eyes-off-my-woman look. Joe kept looking.

Tyler understood why. Lilah was no man's woman. Yet. But after today there would be many men trying for her.

He tried to block out the crowd. He did his best to block her from view by moving in front of her.

"Maybe we should go inside," he said.

She shook her head. "I want to talk, and I want to talk where everyone can hear us."

"You have something to say, then."

She nodded slowly.

He didn't have the slightest idea what she wanted to say, but he knew he wasn't going to like it.

Lilah looked up at him in challenge.

"The last two times I saw you, you were putting on a show. You weren't being yourself."

He didn't say anything. Whatever he said would come out wrong, anyway.

She lifted her chin higher. "I know you did that to help me." She turned to the crowd and shrugged. "My brothers wanted to find me a husband. I wanted to find my own. I was tired of being seen as just a nice, complacent woman. Tyler made me look…interesting."

He smiled then. He brushed a hand down her jaw. She raised her head and leaned into his touch, in full view of everyone. "You never needed me to make you look interesting, love. You're the most interesting woman I know."

She wrinkled her nose.

He laughed. "You are."

Her frown deepened, and she crossed her arms beneath her breasts, which only served to lift and accentuate the lovely swell of those barely covered assets of hers.

Tyler shifted his stance when he noticed Phil Eddison trying to get a better look.

"I shouldn't have asked you to help me put on a charade," she said, shaking her head of taffy-colored hair, "but those last few days you went out of your way to change yourself to make a point with me, to show me what you thought I should be looking for in a man. I just wanted everyone to know what you'd tried to do for me, Tyler. And I wanted you to know that if you can change yourself to make a point with me, I can do the same."

She placed her hands on her hips. Her top slipped a notch. He gave up trying to be discreet and, reaching out, slipped his fingers inside her top and pulled it up a bit, his knuckles skimming across the warmth of her skin.

She shivered visibly, but it was nothing compared to what was going on inside him. And it wasn't just the exquisite, revealing sight of her. It was the fire in her eyes, the stubborn set of her chin and those tempting red lips. It was the way she was looking at him as if he was the only one standing here with her, when they were surrounded by a crowd.

"What point are you trying to make, love?" he asked.

She smiled finally, though it was a sad, heartbreaking smile. "My point is that you thought you knew what my ideal man was and you did your best to get him for me. You put aside who and what you are and all your own desires to do that for me."

Her eyes misted over. She looked away for a second, biting her lip, then swung her head back, her eyes glimmering as she faced him again.

"Well, I know what your favorite kind of woman is, too. I know what you've forfeited for me this summer. To help me you gave up all those women who have been wanting you and waiting for you. You gave your summer to a quiet little bookseller when you were surrounded by beautiful, exotic women. Women who know just how to dress and how to whisper in a man's ear. You gave up your time. You changed your plans. You've sacrificed for me."

He opened his mouth.

She placed her fingers over his lips and shook her head.

"No more," she said. "It's time I gave your life back to you. There's still some time left here on the island. You didn't get to do the things you wanted to when you came here as a boy. Well, now you can. You can have your life back. I want people to know that. You're a good man. You're a free man. And you're not *my* man. You should have a woman like this," she said, looking down at herself, "and they're all here, waiting for you."

She looked around at the crowd. He didn't.

Standing here, next to this slender willow of a woman, this usually quiet, retiring woman, he was aware that Lilah had made her point. People were murmuring, no doubt about the fact that he and Lilah had been playing a game all this time. And now she was calling a halt to the game.

She thought she'd deprived him of the things he wanted, but what he wanted was standing in front of him. All he wanted or had ever wanted was right here, and she was cutting him loose, sending him away.

He'd known from the start what kind of man was right for her and that he wasn't it, but here she was saying the words, ending it forever.

Pain swirled through him, clogging his throat, stinging his eyes, making him want to clutch her to him. But he wouldn't do that. She'd come to him looking for freedom to make her own choices, and now she was making a choice.

He nodded slightly. "Come with me?" he asked, holding out his hand.

This time she acquiesced. She took his hand and they went inside her store. She pulled the shades and locked the door.

As soon as she turned to face him, he took a step toward her.

''So...you're calling off our arrangement. Why now?'' he asked, his voice tight and slightly choked.

Lilah looked directly at him through intense, pain-filled eyes. ''Last night, the day before—you're changing yourself for me. I don't want that. Not that. I want you just to be yourself. Always. I like you just as you are.''

Her lips were trembling, tears were gathering in her eyes.

Tyler slipped his arms around her and pulled her to him.

''You like me.'' They were such sweet words, but such hard ones to bear.

She burrowed her head against him, slipped her arms around his waist and nodded. He could feel the tension in her body. How he wanted to hold her, to have her, to be more.

''Like,'' he said, his voice rasping and dull. She raised her head.

In her high heels, her lips were closer than they had been in the past. He took them, covering them with his own, moving in as close as he could get to her, trying to imprint the taste and feel of her on his memory.

And then he pulled back. He thought he saw a touch of regret in her eyes. A shade of something else. And maybe he was just imagining it.

Hoping for something that wasn't there.

''Lilah?'' he asked.

She parted her lips. ''It wasn't my brothers who told you how I felt, was it? It was me...because what I feel for you shows, doesn't it?'' she whispered. ''I'm sorry. I didn't mean to fall in love with you. I don't even want to love you, Tyler. It means we can't be friends anymore, doesn't it?''

A long shudder of relief and release ripped through him.

His legs felt suddenly unsteady, his heart felt as if it would beat its way right out of his chest.

''I'm afraid it does mean we can't be friends,'' he said.

''I knew that.'' Her voice was barely discernible, and his heart both broke for her and spilled over with joy.

Lowering his head, he kissed her lips. Then he lifted her into his arms and kissed her again. Slowly. Deeply. He took what he needed so terribly. What he'd always needed and had never known. This woman, his sweet Lilah had given him his heart, she'd restored his soul.

''Kiss me back,'' he urged.

She did, then broke away as he grinned and reached for her again.

''Tyler, what are you doing? I thought—''

''Lilah, angel,'' he drawled. ''You're a very intelligent woman. Can't you see what I'm doing, love? I'm kissing you. I'm being myself. I'm doing exactly what I want to do.'' And what he wanted to do for the rest of his life.

From her perch in his arms, held against his chest, she reached out and framed his face with her hands.

''I didn't know. We've always played a charade. Is this the way you are with other women when you're being yourself?'' Her voice was hesitant, uncertain.

Instantly he pulled her closer and kissed her softly.

''This is the way I am with one woman. Only one woman. The woman I love. The woman who was once a girl who fascinated me, and the woman who may have been invisible to others, but who was never invisible to *me.*''

Lilah's heart took wing. It seemed to fly up to the sun and come home again as she gazed into the eyes of the man she loved with such sweet intensity.

She smiled and touched her lips to his gently. ''Ah, but you're an extraordinary man, Tyler, the most extraordinary man I've ever met. Not every man sees the things you see, and not every man can do the things you do.''

''I hope not,'' he said against her lips. ''I don't want any other man holding you or touching you or making love to you. I want to be the only man with the right to your bed, and the man you decide to marry. You may not want to change me, Lilah, but you already have. You've made me feel what I've never felt.''

''You're sure? This wasn't what I'd planned today, you know,'' she said.

''I can see that,'' he said with a smile, looking down at her red stretchy top and sliding one hand along her bare thigh where her skirt had ridden up. Your plan was to drive every man in town wild with lust.''

''Tyler…''

''Say you love me again.''

''Tyler, I love you. I adore you. I've adored you from the first moment I ever saw you.'' She knew that now. She'd been looking for the right man, but there had only ever been one man who filled her soul with light, one man who made her whole, one man who felt like home.

He groaned low in his throat. ''I wish I'd acted on my inclinations when we were young and approached you then.''

She shook her head slowly. ''Maybe we had to live

a lot to get to this. Maybe this is better.'' Tears filled her eyes as she realized that nothing could be better than this. Tyler loved her and she loved him, and this time there was no pretending, only joy.

She kissed him then, long and deep, wrapping her arms around him as he leaned against the wall and slid to the floor with her, shifting her onto his lap.

''This is…extraordinary,'' he said on a groan. ''The best moment of my life. You're probably right about the road we took to get here, Lilah, because this summer you taught me to love. As it is, I'm even looking forward to doing all that community service I'll owe you for not fulfilling our bargain of finding you that perfect man you were looking for. I'm not perfect, Lilah, but I dare any man to say he loves you more than I do. I challenge any man to try and step in to take my place.''

She kissed his jaw. ''You don't have to do community service. You did help me find the man I wanted,'' she confessed.

''Mmm, not the same,'' he said, nuzzling her neck. ''I'm not the kind of man you intended, and I'll do my community service gladly. Later. After I've kissed you maybe a thousand times. After you've married me.''

Lilah pushed up off his chest and stared into his eyes, her own dark and serious. ''You should know something, Tyler. You've changed me, too. I thought I just wanted an ordinary man, but I guess I lied. I only want you. I think I've always wanted you.''

He smiled and pulled her close to his heart. ''Lilah, my only love,'' he drawled. ''There's not a man alive who would feel ordinary with you in his arms. I'm going to spend my life showing you just how special you make me feel. It's going to be my very greatest pleasure. You can bet on that. You can name any price you please. This is one bet I'll never lose.''

And to seal his wager, he took another kiss.

Epilogue

The bookstore was empty. It was the perfect time. Lilah looked up into her husband's face.

"Are you braced?" she asked. "I've got news."

He raised a brow. "Sounds serious. You've just found one of those rare tomes of history you've been searching out for me?"

Lilah chuckled. She lightly tapped her husband on the arm and noticed that he was staring down at her abdomen.

"You know already, don't you?"

He shrugged and pulled her close. "I guessed. You've been humming a lot lately. Lullabies. A beautiful sound."

She couldn't keep the worry from her eyes in spite of her words. "It's only been a little over a year since Rose was born. We've only been married two years. You're…happy with the news."

He smiled and pulled her closer, kissing the top of

her head. "More than happy. I'm ecstatic, and why shouldn't I be?"

"Not all men would be."

"Some men don't know a good thing when they see it," he said, looking pointedly at her. "If the men in Sloane's Cove had been smart, one of them would have coaxed you into giving up your freedom long before I came along. As it is, I got everything. My stepbrother's restaurant is thriving, I've opened my own. Your bookstore is a hive of activity, Rose is all a man could want in a daughter, and now you've made me the happiest of men. All over again, love," he whispered.

"I'm glad, then," she whispered back, running her fingers into his hair. "You don't miss your life of adventure, now and then?"

He pulled back and grinned wickedly. "Who says I've given up my life of adventure? I was thinking of doing something exciting with my wife this very afternoon. Something involving a bed and a boat and the rocking of the waves."

"Sounds positively wicked and wonderful," she said, wrapping her arms around his neck. "But weren't you supposed to be giving a presentation of some sort in your restaurant today? Wasn't I supposed to be selling books?"

He kissed the sensitive spot just under her jaw, tipping her head back and nudging her up against a bookshelf. "I guess people will just have to wait to buy books. I'll just be a bit late for my presentation. After all, love, when a woman gives a man a gift such as you've just given me, he's expected to thank her in the best way he knows how. That man would want to show her that he worships the very air she breathes."

Lilah wasn't sure she was even breathing anymore.

"Kiss me again," she whispered.

"And again," he agreed, doing just that. "Is there anything more important than two people who love each other celebrating the impending arrival of a child who is the product of that love?"

He pulled back and waited for her answer.

She brought her lips within a breath of his own. "There's nothing more important than that, my love," she whispered, and she slipped from beneath his arms and moved to the door to flip the Open sign to Closed. It was a slow day with the season ending. Natalie had gone back to college. There was no one to mind the store.

Smiling at two potential customers who were nearing the store, she waved as she held her hand out to Tyler and opened the door.

"I'm sorry," she said, indicating the sign, "but my husband and I are having a celebration today."

"Another baby?" one of the woman asked with a smile. "That man," she said, but there was a trace of admiration in her voice.

"That man," Lilah agreed, as Tyler came up behind her, looped his arm around her waist and drew her close. "I love him, but he *is* a bit wicked, isn't he?"

Tyler laughed and brought his lips near her ear. "He's just a man in love with his wife, sweetheart. Absolutely, completely in love with his wife."

Lilah turned to him, ignoring her customers. "And his wife is very much in love with him, too," she said softly.

"Was there ever such a wonderful woman?" he asked the ladies as Lilah closed up shop and he drew her close to lead her down the street. "And to think that I might have missed you if I'd never come to restore my home,'' he said.

''To think that I might have married someone else if I'd listened to my brothers,'' she agreed.

He stopped dead in the street and drew her near to face him. ''You wouldn't have,'' he whispered, his voice low and fierce, and she knew that very thought had occurred to him before.

''No, I wouldn't have,'' she whispered to him. ''Because I was waiting for you, even if I didn't know it.''

He smiled gently and slid his hand up through her hair, cupping her neck. ''Thank you, my love,'' he said. ''For waiting.''

Drawing her slowly to him, he kissed her. Softly. Reverently. A mere brushing of lips. A promise. ''Thank you for making a home for me in your heart.''

He slid his hand up over her heart. She knew that it was beating very fast. He always had that effect on her.

''Tyler?'' she whispered, swallowing hard.

''Yes?''

She managed a weak grin. ''If you don't want your wife to earn a reputation as a notorious woman who behaves brazenly with her husband in the middle of the street, you'd better lead me to our boat and our bed.''

He chuckled softly. He kissed her long and hard.

Hours later Lilah turned in Tyler's arms. She raised up and smiled down into his eyes, her hair falling in a silky curtain around them.

''My brothers don't know what they nearly deprived me of.''

Tyler smiled up at her, tucking her hair behind her ears and framing her face with his hands. ''Maybe they were just getting you ready for marriage. For me. The

Austin brothers and I have grown to like each other, you know.''

''I know,'' she said softly. ''I'm glad.''

''How glad?'' he asked, and his voice was thick, his fingers on her skin were urgent.

''I can't tell you how much,'' she whispered. ''It's too much to tell. But I can show you.''

And she brought her lips down to her husband's. He pulled her into his arms and turned her beneath him.

''Show me, love,'' he whispered. ''Show me again.'' His lips descended to hers.

Lilah wrapped her arms around the man she had chosen, the only man her heart would have.

''Yes. Again,'' she whispered.

* * * * *